I want to thank all of my friends, family, neighbors, and even enemies, for inspiring me:

To Ocie Grimsley, my beautiful queen, for being my motivation and my publisher, in one way or another

To my parents Molly and Christopher Carr, for putting up with all my crazy ramblings as I attempted to explain my story ideas, or zoned out during a conversation to randomly start drumming my fingers as I thought out the next plot twist

And above all, I want to express my deepest gratitude to you, the person who is reading this novel, for spending your money on my story and helping to make a crazy eighth-grader's dream a reality

-J.C.

Part One: Rise of the Dark King

Chapter 1

Date: November 27th, 2111
Time: 0245Z hours Zulu Time, 1045 hours local time
Place: Base Camp Delta, Southern Komodo Island

I'm Brigadier General Jack Maxus Marr of the Earth-Space Special Forces, and this is where my real story begins.

I was sleeping peacefully that morning when one of the privates began to knock on my door, the same one that had been forced to come wake up the 'Terror of Nevada' every day since my arrival.

"What is it Private Thomas?" I called out.

"Ha-how did you know it was me, sir?" Thomas stuttered nervously.

"One," I spoke through gritted teeth, "When you knock, you sound like you think you might break a nail. Two, you always lose the arm wrestling game they play to see who has to wake me up. And three, you just told me."

I've had already had this conversation with the private several times and knew what he looked like outside the door. He was about five foot five, with blonde hair and a lanky toothpick-like body that was constantly trembling whenever he was within ten feet of me.

"Well, sir, the new cadets are here and most of them are extremely excited to meet you," he said.

"Fine," I grumbled. "Guess it's time to rough up some new rookies. I still hate command for making me do this."

I got dressed in my black Under Amour t-shirt, camouflage jacket, and matching camouflage pants. Then I put on my hat and wrap-around sunglasses, slipped into my boots, and headed out the door towards Private Thomas and the waiting car. The only thing I had that I wasn't supposed to have, at least on my person when I met the recruits, was my special handmade pistol that had a set of small saw blades along the top of the barrel and stood to me as a constant reminder of my dark and bloody history.

"Time to get some losers together and make a new squad, fun for me," I thought angrily. I hated working with other people, but not as much as I hated command for making me do it.

As we drove slowly in front of all the new rookies in perfect formation, I still couldn't believe that I was going to have to pick three of these stuck up snobs and work with them. That's when I saw him: Cadet Number 42. He was slouched, out of formation, and sharpening a switchblade. The kid was at least five foot seven and slightly muscular for his age, which I guessed to be at least twenty-six years old. He had a slight tan that made it look like he had spent the last three days in Hawaii and long, dark brown hair that almost covered his mysterious dark green eyes. We stopped in front of him and slowly stepped out of the car.

"Hey kid, no blades allowed. Hand it over," I said. Then I turned to the private and made him start to tremble again as I glared at him. "Didn't you search him before you took off? Make sure I was the only threat to any of the cadets?" I said, only slightly joking as I stared blankly at him and awaited an answer.

"Yes sir. We searched him and found three switchblades in his jacket lining, two throwing daggers tucked into each boot, and a .3mm handgun tucked into the small of his back in his belt that he said was in case things got ugly." The private stammered in his shaky, girly voice as he wrapped his arms tightly around himself in an attempt to stop his body from shaking.

"All right kid," I said, my tone clearly showing that I was done playing around and wanted to get on with what I had to do as I turned my attention from Private Thomas and back to the kid with the knife. "How'd you get that one past the super-searcher?"

"Easy, it's not mine, it's his." He replied in a bored tone, pointing it at the private and revealing the pathetic hot pink handle of the serrated blade.

"Well game's over. Give it back," I said flatly.

"Or what, you'll use your little blade pistol?" He teased as he pulled out my pistol and started playing with the blades above the barrel with a stupid grin.

What happened next would have looked to any of the cadets watching like I had teleported. In less than a second I was behind him and had him in a suffocating submissive hold, his face covered by my thick arm as I applied a gradually increasing amount of pressure to his throat. When I let go, he collapsed to the sand as he gagged, coughed, wheezed, and struggled to regain his normal breathing pattern while his windpipe began to retake its original shape.

"You want this stupid pistol so bad? Let's wrestle for it," he said between gasps, not knowing the big mistake he just made.

"You've got yourself a deal there kid." I said with my first smile since my plane touched down on the island.

I had been waiting for something like this for a long time. This is going to be fun.

As we shook on the fight, the kid, whose name, according to the roster, was Alexander Griffen, said, "Since you obviously have more experience in hand-to-hand combat, you have to wear a handicap vest."

"Sure," I said. "How much weight should it be?"

"Let's see, how about you have a one hundred fifty pound handicap. A one-fifty pound vest," he repeated, more sure the second time.

"One fifty! That's it? Let's do three hundred pounds, if that's ok with you little girl," I sneered.

"Fine, 300 pounds it is. It's your funeral," he said.

"Actually, I believe it's more likely yours kid. I hope you've picked out a coffin. Otherwise you'll just get a simple thing of just a mound of sand with some driftwood tied together to form a cross on them, and the Komodo dragons that live here usually dig up the bodies and eat the leftovers," I said in reply. Then I turned to the private and loudly barked, "Thomas! Go get my 300 pound vest. And get someone to help you since you have trouble picking up a Desert Eagle, and that only weighs four pounds!"

Chapter 2

When the private got back, the other rookies had made a circle in the sand where the fight would take place. I heard a few of them gasp when I slipped on the vest as if it weighed nothing at all and couldn't help but chuckle softly to myself. After I clipped on the straps for the vest, I headed for the ring. When we were both ready for the fight, he took his shirt off and tried to look tough. As he took his off, some girls seemed impressed. Just because I felt like reciprocating the stupid tough-guy gesture, I ripped my shirt off under the vest. However, when I took mine off and exposed my large and muscular chest that was covered in all different sorts of scars and wounds, the air filled with an audible gasp that seemed to come from everyone instead of just a single person. Alex even looked a little dizzy and trembled slightly before clenching his fists tightly to regain control over himself. Now it was time for what we had all been waiting for: the fight. We started going around the outside of the ring as the crowd watched with bated breath.

"What are you waiting for? Make your move, you little pussy." I sneered tauntingly.

He lunged forward quickly and attempted to throw a right jab to my face. That was his first, and last, mistake Just as he was about to hit me, I caught his fist, gripped it tightly for added pain and effect, twisted it around behind his back, kicked his feet out from under him, and pushed his body against the beach sand with one hand while pulling his right arm up behind his back, utilizing a technique I had learned and mastered long ago that one of my friends had nicknamed 'the chicken wing,' until the young man howled in pain and tapped out with his other hand.

"What a waste of my time. Now, on to real business," I said as I took back the switchblade that said "I Love my Mommy" on it in cute red letters and my Blood Pistol from where he had stashed it on his belt, released his right arm, and walked back to Private Thomas as Alex curled into a tight ball around his injured arm and sobbed softly. I tossed the private his switchblade, which he juggled to try and catch before it fell to the ground, and tucked my pistol back in its holster in the small of my back. Then I turned back to the cadets, who were standing at a slight distance from Alex, and gave them their first set of instructions, ignoring the menacing look in Alex's eyes.

"Now that we've established who's in command here," I said clearly to get the cadets' attentions again, "we will begin the process to see who will be chosen to follow me around as my squad. Ten miles up the beach, you will find two large, square mounds in the sand. Our tests will start there. I don't recommend kicking the mounds, or you will be in for a painful and rusty surprise. In each mound there are one hundred rusted machetes placed as a gift from the locals, and we ran out of tetanus shots last week. Now GO GO GO!!!!!!!!!!!!"

When the slowest cadets had finally arrived, I began to bark out the next set of orders for them, some of whom were still struggling to catch their breath after the run.

"Today," I began somewhat overdramatically, "You will be taking a basic pushup test. You will be doing the original old-fashion pushup. The same kind of testing that I had to do when I was a cadet, many years ago. By the time this is over, most of you will either have dropped out or have been eliminated. Good luck, because if you drop out or are eliminated, there are 'do-over's'. No pressure though, now line up behind the mounds. For this test you will be put into groups of two," I continued. "Once you are all in groups, you will line up around your mounds. One member of the group will get into pushup position and the other will observe and make sure that they are doing the pushups correctly. If they are not, report it to me immediately so that I can eliminate them. If any of the groups are caught hiding incorrect pushups, then both members will be eliminated. Do I make myself clear!?"

"Sir yes sir!" They all shouted back.

"Good," I declared bluntly.

Now with them all in attention, the private and I went through them and put them into pairs. Once the pairs were established, they scurried to line up behind one of the two mounds of sand, and the first test began.

When they finished the pushup test two hours later, at least twenty five of the fifty that started had been either eliminated or had dropped out.

"Now it's time for the sit up test!" I said in a false cheery tone. "You have three minutes to rest, starting now."

"Yes sir," several of the cadets mumbled tiredly, taking as much advantage of the short break time they had been given as possible.

When they finished the sit up test, another ten had dropped out or been eliminated. I hadn't really kept very good track of who had dropped out on their own and who had been eliminated. However, I noticed at the time that the sun had begun to set and that the large Komodo Dragons that inhabited the island would soon emerge to hunt, and since they were about as long as some of the cadets were tall and which would make this even more difficult, and possibly just the slightest bit illegal, even by military standards, that it would be the perfect time to stop for the day.

"That concludes today's assessments. Private, show them to their quarters. Wake-up is 0700 hours and if you're not awake at roll call, you're out. Dismissed," I ordered flatly.

As the private showed the remaining cadets to their quarters, girls in barrack 9a and boys in barrack 5b, I made my way to my private cabin in the jungle and fell on to my bed when I got there, causing the entire cabin to shake slightly. When I rolled onto my back, I stared up at the wall and thought about what the cadets were in for tomorrow. I laughed just thinking about the challenges they faced ahead, then my smile faded at the thought of why they were doing this in the first place, which reminded me of my wife Elana and how she had died to save my life in battle. Eventually I fell into an uneasy sleep that caused several tremors to shake the island during the night.

Chapter 3

By the time Private Thomas had woken all the cadets and me and gotten us all together, it was 0815 hours and I was drinking a cup of black coffee.

"OK kiddies," I said in a flat, sarcastic tone. "Listen up. Today we will be continuing our series of assessments to determine who will be in my squad. We are going to run a series of obstacle courses until one group of three is left. But before we start the courses and put you into groups, I want to call roll to see who is left. Marcus?"

"Here," A blonde twenty-six year old cadet with mild stubble and clear blue eyes said calmly. The expression on his face seemed to show that he really didn't care about still being here. In fact, it didn't really seem like he cared about anything. He was just staring off into space.

"Justin?"

"Present," said the next cadet, who had dark hazel eyes with flecks of gold. He looked like he couldn't have been more than twenty years old, even though I knew that the youngest person here was twenty-four years old. Still, the lack of facial hair, the crew cut, and the basic facial architecture along with his somewhat slender build made him appear to be closer to his late teens in age than mid-twenties.

"I know Alex is here, Eli?"

"Here, ready and willing to serve you!" A somewhat short but stocky cadet with short, curly brown hair and a bright-eyed perky facial expression said in an annoyingly happy tone as he tried to jump and waved his arm to try and get more attention. "Do you need anything? I can find some food or run and get something-"

"No, just shut the fuck up." I growled before returning to the roll call. "Robert?"

"Here," a cadet near the back said in a firm, confident tone. This cadet was probably around thirty years old and seemed confident and yet still friendly at the same time with dark brown hair and lighter brown eyes.

"Jon?"

"Here," a cadet with short brown hair that was about twenty-seven years old and was somewhat muscular, maybe just a little less than Alex, barked from behind Marcus, who jumped at Jon's response.

"Christopher?"

"Here," A blonde-haired cadet that was of average height and build said in a clear tone, staring directly at me when I looked up at him.

"Jason?"

"Here, and I go by Max," a cadet with blonde spiked-up hair and bright green eyes said, his hair the only thing visible of him from where he was standing in the back row.

"Yeah, and I don't care. Joshua?"

"Here," a cadet near the back said somewhat softly, looking down and away as I looked up to make sure someone had answered.

"And last of the boys, Andreas?"

"Present," the tanned cadet answered from the middle of the group with a distinct Hispanic accent. He was around twenty-eight years old and had short, gelled black hair and thick dark stubble on his chin.

"Now for the girls. Jasmine?"

"Here," a pretty blonde with brown eyes answered from the middle. She looked somewhat young too, and seemed like the kind of girl that could get whatever she wanted by flirting with the right boys.

"Venus?"

"Present," A girl with somewhat of an Italian accent said from somewhere in the middle as well, but she must have been too short because it seemed like her answer came between two other girls were standing.

"Roxana?"

"Here," A dark-skinned girl said from the back row. She was somewhat larger in build than the other girls and had an accent that sounded like it came from somewhere in Western Africa.

"Alexandra?"

"Here," a somewhat pale red-head answered from the front of the group. She was a little taller but quite thin in build, and was probably around twenty-five years old.

"And last but not least, Jessica?"

"Here," said the last cadet in a cocky voice. She was near the back of the group as well and stood out because she had hair that was dyed bright red along the edges and then a dark navy blue in the middle area.

"Finally," I said. "Now to put you into groups. Let me think about this, how about Jasmine, Alex and Jason. You three will be Alpha squad."

"Just great," I heard Alex groan.

"Get over it bitch." I growled at Alex, who just glared back at me. "Now, let's see, Marcus you're with Venus and Jon and you will be Beta Squad."

"Um, okay. Sure. Yes sir." Marcus said somewhat timidly but had a week smile on his face as Venus glared at him from behind and Jon gently took Venus's hand. I could easily guess the most probable story behind these three almost instantly. Marcus had probably been dating Venus, who dumped him for Jon, so while Marcus is all too happy to be paired up with his ex, Venus and Jon probably don't want to have anything to do with Marcus.

"Roxana," I went on as I stifled a chuckle at Beta Squad's situation, "You're with Joshua and Robert, and you three will be Omega Squad."

"Ooh, that's a cool name. I like it." Robert chuckled.

"Me two, don't you Josh?" Roxana chuckled, and Joshua just responded with a nod and a smile.

This group was even easier to read than Beta Squad. The three were obviously friends from a long time ago, and Roxana and Robert had probably just started dating. Little to their knowledge, Joshua probably had a huge crush on Roxana that he had been hiding for a while, but he didn't dare say anything that might upset the happy couple. So instead, Joshua became the silent, happy third wheeling wallet.

"Next, Alexandra will be teamed up with Andreas and Christopher as Delta Squad." I decided. This group was nothing special. The three people obviously had nothing in common and didn't know each other at all. "Lastly, Jessica, Eli, and Justin, you three are Zeta Squad." I finished. As with most of the other groups, it was easy to guess the situation of the group. Jessica stood slightly in front of the boys, so she didn't notice her glaring at her multi-colored head. Eli and Justin must have both dated Jessica at some point in time, maybe at the same time, and then she dumped both of them for what appeared to be Andreas based on the looks she was casting towards him. So while Jessica just felt bad for not being on the same time as her new boyfriend, she was completely oblivious to the rage shared by the two boys on her team that was all aimed at her.

"The order will be Omega, then Zeta, then Beta, then Delta, and Alpha will be last. Now get in line and listen up while I explain the obstacle course to you. This course was especially designed to simulate all the different scenarios that the modern soldier would have to face. It should be easy since I do it every day in the morning after my coffee. Because of the military's legal department, which I personally didn't even know existed until about a week ago, I am required not only to lower the challenge level from its max at ten, which is what I do in the morning, to five, which is very simple and the average difficulty. I also am required to save you in case something happens, like if you fall in the shark tank below the monkey bars or the fire pit under the balance beam that was turned into a boiling hot water tank because of the change in difficulty. Here is what you will have to do in order to pass. You will climb up this wooden wall, use the monkey bars to cross the tank that is infested with several species of sharks and piranhas, swing over a pit of sharp spikes to the balance beam, cross the balance beam without falling into the boiling water, cross the rope bridge while dodging energy beams and falling rocks, jump to the ledge on the other side, and jump off the ledge that is 3000 feet in the air, before parachuting safely to the big red 'X' at the end to stop the clock. The clock will only stop when all three of the squad members are standing on it at the same time. Now, line up in your new squads from shortest to tallest and get ready for the obstacle course. Omega Squad, line up on the line, and the rest of you, follow me," I said, leading the other squads up to the observation platform. Once the other squads had joined me on the observation platform suspended on a wall to the left of the obstacle course, I continued my instructions. "Once all three members of Omega Squad are on the white line, I will shout go and the clock will start. You are not allowed to use any equipment whatsoever aside from the parachute at the end of the course. Cheating of any kind will be caused for immediate disqualification of the entire squad. In the end, the fastest three times will move on and the rest will be eliminated. Ready, begin!" I shouted through the intercom so Omega Squad heard it.

And with that the clock started and the first group began the obstacle course.

Chapter 4

By the time Omega Squad had finished, Roxana had been slightly burned and Joshua had a piranha stuck on the ankle of his boot. As they landed on the 'X' and stopped the clock, I reached them and yanked the piranha off Joshua's ankle and tossed it backwards over my shoulder back in its tank, yelling out their time over Joshua's wail of pain from having the piranha yanked off his heel so abruptly.

"Nine minutes and thirty-six seconds is your time. Now the rest of you have to try and beat that to stay in the running. Next up is Zeta Squad. Zeta Squad, come down here and line up at the white line. Omega Squad, head over to the nurse's outpost over there and then head up to meet with the other groups and me in the observation platform." I led Omega Squad up to the observation platform and looked back to cue the next wave. "Zeta Squad ready?" I asked through the intercom, and then without waiting for a reply continued in saying: "On your marks, get set, GO!"

After all the other squads had gone, it was finally time for Alpha Squad to go. Zeta Squad had gotten eight minutes and fifty-five seconds, Beta had gotten seven minutes and thirty-six seconds, and Delta had nine minutes and thirty five seconds. Also, out of the people that had gone, six of them were partially singed and I was a bit nervous about this squad since there seemed to be a lot of tension, which was both good and bad since it also reminded me of my squad that I used to have. I quickly put that memory out of my head so that none of the cadets would notice the sad look in my eyes and visualize it as a sign of weakness.

"Ready, GO!" I shouted.

The clock had just started when Alex put on a burst of speed, separating himself from the rest of the squad. As they hurried to catch up, Alex had already quickly scaled the climbing wall and had begun to cross the monkey bars. Suddenly, his hand slipped off the bar, clearly catching him off guard as he struggled to maintain his grip with his other hand. He lost his grip and began to fall into the shark tank when Jasmine suddenly grabbed his outstretched hand. That gave Jason time to grab his other hand and they worked together to pull him back up. I saw Alex nod a thank-you and they were on their way again. They were almost across the bridge when Jasmine was suddenly struck in the leg by a large fragment of one of the falling rocks and stumbled to the floor. She tried to get up, but she had clearly been hit on a nerve cluster which temporarily cut off all control of her left leg from the knee down. She struggled to get to her feet and keep going, but she had barely taken more than two or three steps before her left leg buckled and she collapsed again. She started to try crawling to the end of the bridge when Alex ran back to her, scooped her up with ease, and carried her across the rest of the bridge like a firefighter. I was waiting for them at the 'X' as Alex strapped on Jasmine's parachute, then his own, and they all jumped together and parachuted down onto the 'X'. They landed at almost the same time and looked at the clock to face their fates and found their time was nine minutes, thirty-two seconds. They had made it by three seconds.

"Alpha Squad, you made it. You are in the top three times and I will see you with Zeta Squad and Beta Squad tomorrow for the final assessments. Delta, Omega, your times were the two lowest. Pack your bags and head back to the airstrip." I said, repeating the words my leader had said to our set of squads what seemed like an eternity ago. They had made it. And I had a feeling about this "Alpha Squad", a feeling of déjà vu. I was probably about as anxious about tomorrow as the other groups were nervous. I couldn't wait for tomorrow to come. I didn't fall asleep until 0500 hours the next morning, and the wakeup time was 0630.

The next morning was the last day of assessments. The cadets would be running a second obstacle course and the victors today would be the ones who I would choose to serve with me in the battles ahead.

"Attention!" I shouted at the cadets. "Today is the final day of assessments to determine the makings of my new team. The groups for the final obstacle course will be the same as yesterday. Today though, we not only will be testing your athletic skills and maneuverability, but we will also be testing your reflexes and accuracy. Yes, today you will be using some of the technology that you will get to use if you are in my squad. You will be firing the standard M25A9 assault rifle. You will also be using the old fashion Desert Eagle .50 AE caliber pistol, and you will be firing at robotic simulations that will be armed and firing back at you. Don't worry; the guns are shooting high velocity paintball imitation rounds, not real bullets. It will hurt though, a lot, and probably leave a large bruise that will last for about a month. Today you will be running the same obstacle course as yesterday, except for today it is on Level 7, which will be slightly more difficult and have the targets. Your guns will be given to you right before the beginning of the course. Also, your score will be a combined total of your time and how many hits you get. Five points for each target hit down, ten points if the hit is a headshot and one point if it is a hit, but the target doesn't go down. Your score from your time will be the time turned into a negative number and subtracted from your points scored by your shots. For example, if you get nine point seventy-five as your time and you get fifty points from shooting, then you would round nine point seventy-five up to ten and then subtract ten from fifty, and then your total would be forty points. The group with the highest points wins. The order will be based on the scores you got yesterday. So Beta will go first, then Zeta, and Alpha will go last again. Same deal as yesterday. Beta, line up on the line, the rest of you stay here in the observation platform and I will be waiting for each squad at the end of the course."

◆ ◆ ◆

    At the end of the final challenge, all the teams had clearly tried their hardest, and some of them would have marks that would follow them for the rest of their life, or at least for a few months. Even so, there was only space for one team to be selected, and the choice had been made.
    "Attention!" I said, causing all of the cadets, aside from Alex, as usual, to straighten up and watch me. "It is my duty to inform you that the results have been looked at and I have made my decision based on the

results. The cadets who have been recruited to be my team and who will fight by my side in the future are as follows: Jason Talon, Alexander Griffen, and Jasmine Rivers. As for the rest of you, I have sent word out to some of my old comrades and they said they could use some new recruits. Pack your things and head out to the airfield and wait for the pilot to come by and pick you up. Alpha Squad, follow me and I'll show you where you will be staying until we get called out." I said. I could see the disappointment in the other cadets' eyes and that Alpha Squad was beaming with pride. Jasmine looked a bit like she was about to pass out from all the excitement. As the other cadets started to make their way out of the door they had came through, my new squad followed me out another door. The tests they had just finished decided that they were my squad, but the tests I knew were ahead would decide how they would be fighting alongside me.

Chapter 5

"Alright! Time for the next set of tests, but first, we need to go to our base," I told my new squad, as I pulled out a radio and pushed the red button on it.

"Black Fox One this is Smasher 97 requesting a Shadow Hawk Squad in area 90078. Please respond," I spoke into the radio. There was a blast of static followed by a man's voice saying:

"Roger that Smasher 97, Shadow Hawk Squad 852 in your vicinity and he is on his way with an escort. I am patching him through to you now."

"Squad Leader 852, I need a Shadow Hawk pick up in sector 90078." I told the pilot, "You will be picking up three cadets and a large man wearing camouflage jacket and pants on the secondary runway. Do not, I repeat do not, attempt to land on primary runway, over."

"Roger that sir. We are in sight and will be landing soon," the radio spat out.

Seconds later I heard the sound of a pair of jet engines and a pair of massive propeller blades. I heard the cadets behind me gasp in awe as a large, black, heavily armed gunship slowly lowered itself down onto the runway. The cockpit hatch opened and an average sized man jumped out onto the ground and immediately stood in attention when he saw me.

"Good afternoon sir," the man said.

"At ease, Sergeant Cross," I replied. The man relaxed and opened the doors into the cargo area where we would be sitting.

"All right, everybody into the Shadow Hawk. This is our ride to base." I ordered.

In no time, everybody was on board and we were in the air. The cadets had their faces pressed against the windows, watching the fighter jets that were called Night Foxes that were our escort.

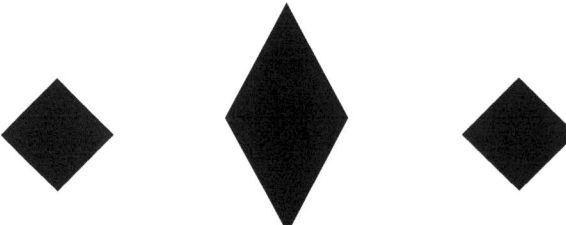

About a half an hour later, we had finally arrived at base. I woke the cadets and waited for the hanger doors to open. As soon as I stepped out, I was shocked to see that all of the people who worked with me at the base were standing just outside of the hanger doors waiting for me.

"Attention!" I shouted, and they all straightened up and stared at me.

"At ease. As you know, I was sent to Komodo Island in order to form a new squad, and I have. Meet my new squad: Jasmine Rivers, Alex Griffen, and Jason Talon!"

As I called out their names, they stepped out to a round of thunderous applause from the troops outside.

"Alright, that's all for now, but you can introduce yourselves to them later after I show them around. Now, move! Let's get to work!" I ordered, the small smile disappearing off my face and I began to march inside.

"SIR YES SIR!" They shouted in reply.

As the crowd marched back into the base, the cadets and I went in after them so I could show them their new home. I gave them the grand tour and showed them their quarters, the weapons chamber, the landing pad, which was also used as a hanger, and the command center, where I explained that the base could, if necessary, shift into a large tank-like vehicle that had a top speed of 300 miles per hour.

"That concludes our tour of our base. There is just one thing we have to agree on before we go any farther: a squad name. I have an idea, but I need you three to agree with it before we can use it. Shadowstar Squad. You like that?"

"That name has a nice ring to it. I say we use it," Jason replied.

"I agree," Jasmine said, nodding.

"I guess it could work," agreed Alex.

"Then it is official. Our name is Shadowstar Squad." I said triumphantly.

"You three should go and meet the rest of the troops. I'm going to take a nap. See you tomorrow morning," I said with a yawn.

"Alright, see you tomorrow, sir," said Jasmine as they all walked away towards the mess hall where the rest of the troops were waiting for them.

As I made my way to my quarters, I thought about how much trouble these kids would face in the war ahead. I fell onto my bed and began to drift into a deep sleep.

Chapter 6

The next morning, I woke up, got dressed, and headed up to the control room. I put in the pass code, 43961, and the door slide open.

"Good morning sir." The private said without even looking up from his screen.

"Morning private, where is the PA system? I forgot where it was since they didn't have one over on Komodo," I said blankly.

"On the front control panel, middle microphone, second blue button from the left," the private replied.

"Thanks, and I push these buttons to direct which rooms hear it, right?" I asked.

"Yes sir. Waking up the new rookies?" he asked.

"Do you know me or what?" I replied with a chuckle.

I pushed the button and an energy screen that was a floor plan of the sleeping quarters popped out from a small projector. I tapped the rooms A4, D7, and F10, which I knew were the cadets' rooms, picked up the receiver, pressed the second blue button from the left, and shouted into the receiver:

"WAKE UP SOLDIERS! TO THE MESS HALL NOW! I WANT YOU DOWN THERE AND EATING BREAKFAST IN THREE MINUTES! GO! GO! GO!" I smiled to the private as he looked up at me from his control panel.

"I love my job!" I said with a snicker.

The guys were there in the mess hall a minute later, and Jasmine was there another minute and a half later. They were all eating their breakfast of cereal so fast that I was worried they would choke on it. After they had finished their breakfast, I led them to the shooting range in the weapons chamber.

When we got there and I had them line up in front of me, I took a second to look over my new squad. Jasmine was very limber looking and slim with the slightest bit of muscle. She had medium length blonde flowing hair and beautiful, warm brown eyes. Jason looked very much like the average soldier in his height and build. The only real things that stood out about him were his spiky and flamboyant blonde hair and his piercing bright green eyes.

"You remember when I said that we were a squad?" I asked the cadets. "Well a squad has many different parts. And today, the tests you will take will decide what part each of you will be. My hope is that we will be evenly distributed so that one of you is the artillery gunner, who handles the explosives, and mortars, as well as light and heavy machine guns and anti-aircraft weapons. Another will be a stealth sniper, for when we need to stay hidden or when one of us is pinned down, and another will be a standard fighter, who usually uses an assault rifle, shotgun, and pistol. Well, enough chit-chat. Time to start. The first part will determine our artillery gunner. First, you will pick up one of those M350s on the table and use the strap to put it on your back and begin the course. You will make your way around and over a set of obstacles, and then use the M350s to gun down as many targets as possible. Once you are done with that, you will receive a box from me. Each box contains a completely disassembled carbon rod cannon. You will then assemble the cannon before having it inspected by me. If it passes the inspection, you will move on to the final part of the artillery gunner test. We have some scraped parts of some enemy aircraft that have been shot down, tied onto indestructible cables that will be lifted up in the air. You will have to use your cannon to shoot and destroy at least five of the ten targets in five minutes, which means that you will have to reload at least once. You will be scored on both time and accuracy, and the person with the highest score wins the position. The test starts in three…two…one…go!"

A bell rang and they were off. Alex was in front and had already finished strapping on the M350 when the other two got to their guns. Alex and Jason had little to no problems picking up and carrying their M350s. Jasmine wasn't as strong as they were though and had trouble lifting it. By the time she had started the obstacle course, the boys were almost done, so I headed over to give them the next challenge. I noticed immediately that Alex was having no problem whatsoever shooting the targets but Jason was struggling with the recoil. When Alex finished with the target course, I gave him the box with the cannon parts in it and he went to work right away. In less than two minutes, he had finished building the cannon and had made it perfectly. I gave him the carbon rods and he loaded the gun like a trained professional, before shooting down all ten targets in three minutes. Alex had a perfect score of one hundred, Jason had a score of eighty six, and Jasmine had a score of seventy three.

"I think it's unanimous who our squad's artillery gunner is. Alex! Since you have your position, you need to practice with what you will be using in the field. Go over into the next room. There is a woman in there named Andrea Jackson. Tell her that you are a new artillery gunner and need to learn the basics. If she doesn't believe you, tell her I sent you. That will get you in. Continue to practice the basics until your teammates here come in and join you. Once they learn the basics of their positions, all three of you will leave and meet me in the hanger." I said. Then, I turned to the other two as Alex left the area.

"Now it's time to find your two positions." I said. "The next tests will determine our team sniper. We will test your skills with both a semi automatic and an automatic sniper rifle. First, you will use the semi automatic rifle to hit the targets that will appear on the opposite side of the target course. Then, you put down the semi automatic rifle and pick up an automatic sniper rifle and make your way through the course while not only dealing with the targets as they appear, but gun challenges, including reloading and possibly a rifle jam. Winner is determined by the amount of points scored. You will earn points based on how many targets you hit, where you hit them, and if they go down. You will also earn points based on your time. If your time is under two minutes, you get one point. If it is under a minute and thirty seconds, you get three points. If it is under a minute, you get ten points. And if it is under thirty seconds, you get twenty extra points. On your marks, get set, go!"

    In no time they were both at the table with the rifles on it and waiting for the targets to pop. The first set came up. They both fired. Jasmine hit the head, fifteen points. Jason hit center mass, ten points. The next popped up, slightly farther away. Both fired. Jasmine hit the head again, thirty points. Jason hit slightly lower in the five point area, fifteen points. The next set popped up, still farther than before, and they were moving. Both fired once more. Jasmine hit the head dead center, forty-five points total, while Jason barely nicked the outside ring that was worth one point. Now the score going into the target course was Jasmine with forty-five points against Jason with sixteen points. Now it was time for the target course. They put down their semi automatic rifles on the table and picked up the automatic rifles. They took their spots on the line and a soundproof barrier dropped down the middle of the target course and made it so Jason and Jasmine would be completely clueless to as where the other person was in the course. The air horn sounded and they started on the course. They started to jog forward when the first targets popped up. Jasmine turned quickly and fired a single shot to the target's head and kept moving, but Jason stopped quickly, crouched, aimed for about two seconds, then finally fired and hit the target's head, then stood up and kept moving. This process repeated the entire time, both before and after they reloaded, although Jason had some trouble reloading because he thought his gun was jammed when he had actually simply forgotten to chamber the first round. Eventually, he figured out his mistake and fixed it, and everything proceeded smoothly for a while. When Jasmine was about halfway through the course and Jason was about a quarter ways through, Jasmine's gun jammed. I thought it was ironic since she had been doing so well so far and the jam was going to cost her the lead. Then I watched in awe as she opened up the gun, fixed the jam, closed the gun, and started moving again in less than half a second. Things went back to the way they were before until they were about to finish the course, and a target that had been set to go off later popped up behind them. Jason jumped in surprise and jerked around quickly, firing his last three shots at the target. Two of them nicked the shoulder areas on the target while the third hit right between the legs. I winced at how that would have felt if it had been a real person. Jasmine's reaction, on the other hand, was as if she had dealt with things like that on a daily basis. Without even looking, she flipped the gun around in her hand, fired at the target, and hit it right between where the eyes should be. Of course, they didn't finish at the same time, so they didn't both react at the same time. Jason's final time was four minutes, fifty two seconds, so he didn't get a bonus, his score going to a total of thirty-five points. Jasmine finished with a stunning ten and a half seconds, even with the gun jam. That gave her an unnecessary twenty point bonus, giving her a whopping score of ninety-two points. I check the data banks, and they confirmed my memory that the only person who had done better on the course since the beginning of the creation of the Earth-Space Branch of the Special Forces was my wife Elana, who had gotten a score of ninety-six points and a time of three and a quarter seconds. I quickly closed the files when I heard the door open and greeted the kids as they came in through the door.

"Congratulations Jasmine. You are our team sniper, which means that you are our foot soldier Jason. Jasmine, you can go and join Alex in the training room while I test what kind of foot soldier Jason will be."

"Yes sir. Thank you sir," Jasmine said.

"Yeah, thanks a lot sir," Jason mumbled.

As Jasmine left, I walked up to Jason as he put his rifle back on the shelf, where some of the privates would come at the end of the day to put it back in the arsenal room.

"Look, I think I know what your problem is Jason. You wanted to be a special part of the group, and you think that being a foot soldier is going to make you common and not an important part. Well let me tell you something, soldier. The foot soldier is just as important as the other parts of the team, if not more important. The foot soldier is the first one in, and usually the last one out. And you want to know a secret?" I asked him as I lowered my voice to a whisper and leaned in close to him.

"What?" He asked curiously as he leaned closer to hear me.

"Don't tell anyone, but I was a foot soldier when I was your rank, and look at where I am now," I said softly.

"Wow. I can't believe it. I might end up like you in the future," Jason said with a surprised look on his face.

"We need to see if you will be a scout or an infantry man. And to speed things along, you should have some competition." I said with a grin, raising my voice.

"But, the other's have already moved on, and I don't want to stop them just for me, so who's....oh!" He said as a look between shock and joy spread across his face.

"I hope you don't just give up because I'm your commanding officer, but don't go easy on me even though I'm a little rusty from my time on Komodo Island. Those blockheads messed up and sent me there a week early and I woke up the next day at 06:00 hours, did two hundred pushups and two hundred sit ups, and was on my way to the airstrip when one of the local privates, Private Thomas, told me in his little girl voice." I made a perfect imitation of Private Thomas's high-pitched girl voice and said: "Uh, sir, I know you are new here but, um, the cadets aren't supposed to come for a-another w-week, sir." Jason and I both started laughing out loud. "Well, I guess we should start. I will do my equivalent of the infantry, then recon scout tests, and you will do the actual tests. And whichever test you do better in is the group you will be in." I turned to the control panel and turned up one side of the course for me, but kept the barrier in place. I took my spot on my side of the course, grabbed the M25A9 off the table and got ready.

"On your mark, get set, GO!" I said and we were off. He couldn't hear me, but I could hear him. He was just unloading wildly on the targets. I was making sure that I used controlled short bursts since unlike him, I only had three seventy-five shot magazines. We both finished at about the same time. He had hit all the targets, five of which he got lucky and hit in the head, but some didn't go down and he didn't stop to check for them, so that would cost him some points. Next was the scout test. This one was harder because the goal wasn't only to knock down the targets, which had been changed from cardboard cutouts to simulation robots that were armed with high velocity paintball guns; you had to do it all without being discovered by any of the other robots. If you were discovered, you would be an automatic target and you wouldn't be able to hide since the robot's thermal sensors would be activated when the alarm was activated. Eventually, after you were hit at least twice by each robot, the course would reset and you would have to restart the entire course from the beginning. We put down our assault rifles and picked up our sub-machine guns and pistols. My guns were a P160 and a Desert Eagle and his were a PDW2 and a Beretta M9. I put on my silencers before helping him get his silencers on all the way. Then we took our places on the lines.

"On your mark, get set, GO!" I said and we were off once more. I got down behind a bunker and heard the first robot guard approaching. Unlike the other test, they had a copy similar to this on Komodo. I saw the guard walk past me and in an instant I fired two shots that went straight into the back of the robot's head. I carried the "body" behind the bunker I had been behind a second ago before moving onto the next barricade. I peeked around the side of the barricade and killed the next two guards up ahead. I ran up to move them out of the way when I noticed a guard coming towards me. We made eye contact, and he was starting to make a break for the alarm button when I fired twice and he dropped like a stone to the ground. I knew that there was one left, and then I remembered something: I had killed two guards at the second barricade. There was supposed to be three. I spun half way around and fired two shots. I saw the last robot, just as he was lifting his hand to press the alarm button. He was about to push it when he was hit by a bullet right between the eyes and dropped like a stone. His hand stayed stuck out and hit the wall just half an inch below the button. The door at the end opened and I lowered my guns before walking through it. Almost as soon as the door I had come through had closed, the other opened and Jason walked out.

"I came really close to being caught," he said, wiping sweat from his brow. "The robot was a step away from the alarm button when I hit him."

"You think you came close?" I asked, raising my eyebrows. "My last robot somehow got past me and when I hit him his hand landed half an inch away from the button as he fell. Anyways, let's see the results." I paused, looking at the results on the computer screen before looking back at Jason. "Looks like you are... an infantry soldier! Just like I was! Go on and join your teammates. I'll see you later in the hanger," I said.

"Sir, yes sir! Thank you, sir!" Jason grinned before heading towards the training room.

About half an hour later I was waiting in the hanger, when the cadets came in talking to each other.

"Attention!" I said.

They immediately stopped talking and straightened up.

"At ease," I said, having now gotten their attentions. "Now that you know your positions in the squad, it's time to put our team to the test. I have been waiting for something like this since we got back, so I had one of the privates in the control center pick a mission that was slightly challenging, but for people who are still working on communication skills. I had him put it on hold for us, and now that we know what kind of guns we are best with, we can finally go out and do a mission. So everybody into the Shadow Hawk and I'll go get the guns and be right back."

The cadets filed into the Shadow Hawk and I went off to the arsenal room to get the guns for the mission ahead. I was so excited for the mission that I almost ran into the door, since it opened slower then I remembered. I couldn't wait to get back in the field again.

Chapter 7

When I had finally gotten all the guns, I raced back to the hanger and sprinted into the Shadow Hawk, nearly trampling an engineer that was working on a Night Fox which looked like it had seen much better days. It was a wonder it had even made it back to the hanger. I ran onto the Shadow Hawk and tapped the side of the plane to tell the pilot that everyone was on board and ready for takeoff. I sat down as we started to take off and felt a rush of energy from hearing the rumbling of the jet engines turn on to replace the propellers and launch us towards our destination.

"Alright," I said. "I have your guns here for you. Alex, you get the Carbon Rod Cannon and the M350 light machine gun. Jasmine, you get the M287 automatic combat sniper rifle and the Jungle Hawk pistol. Max, you get the M25A9 assault rifle and the M2028 shotgun. I get my personally designed Striker-Fi-3 assault rifle, my own M2028 shotgun, and my pistols. Load 'em up, grab some extra ammo, and get ready to land. I still need to brief you real quick. We will be landing near a house that is rumored to house some guards that used to work for a king, that I will not tell you any more about at the time. We will need to breach the house, capture them, and bring them back for interrogation. Any questions?"

"Yes," said Alex. "If we are going into a house, then why do I need the cannon?"

"You need the cannon because they are rumored to have a small jet in the backyard, which they might use as an escape route. If you have to shoot them down, then aim for the engines. You will also use the breaching charge for the back door. You will go through the back door with Max, and I will go in through the front door. Jasmine, you will stay on after we get off and the pilot will take you to a nearby ridge. This is in case they call in reinforcements or try to make a break for it. Alright, we're almost there. Max, Alex, grab one of those breaching charges and check your weapons and ammo. We won't even get a landing. It will be a dust off. I'll get the door."

   I opened the hanger door with my guns strapped onto my back and in my holsters. When we were about three or four feet from the ground, I jumped out, Alex and Max close behind me. Alex had his breaching charge in his hand. I quickly told him how to use it before we split up. Alex went with Max around the house to the back door while I walked up to the front door and placed the charge on it. I took a few steps back, pulled out the transmitter, and flipped the switch. The charge blew the door off its hinges and I ran in before the smoke had even started to clear. I heard another bang as I started up the stairs, telling me that Alex had set off his charge and they were on their way to the top floor on a different set of stairs. When I got to the top floor, I pulled out my Striker-Fi and started towards the end of the hallway. I heard Alex and Max come up and I signaled for them to start checking the other rooms for anyone else. I paused for a second outside of the door at the end of the hall before kicking it down and drawing my assault rifle, keeping my finger off the trigger just in case of innocents.

   "Earth-Space Special forces, nobody move!" I shouted. There were two men on the other side of the room near a stack of money and a window. They slowly raised their hands, and then they did what most criminals in cop movies do. They jumped out the window behind them, smashing through the foggy glass into the area behind the house. I bolted after them and when I looked to see where they had landed, I quickly realized why they weren't worried about jumping. They fell right into their jet, the hatch already open and ready for takeoff. They landed in the seats, closed the hatch, and started to move forward in preparation for takeoff. I vaulted through the window and hit the ground running, literally. I guess it's worth noting that I've previously free fallen from about fifty feet and walked away relatively unscathed, so jumping about ten feet from a window was nothing in comparison. I continued running after the jet, which was rapidly gaining speed was beginning to rise off the ground, and radioed Alex.

"Alex!" I shouted into the radio. "Get outside or to a window ASAP! The targets are in their jet and on the move and heading northwest. I repeat, the targets are on the run heading northwest."

Alex didn't reply. He didn't need to. About thirty seconds later, I saw a flash of green light and a beam of energy shoot out from a top floor window. The shot was dead-on accurate and the hit sent the plane spiraling downward in a steep nosedive. I ran back to the Shadow Hawk and saw Alex and Max come running out of the front door as the plane crashed to the ground about five clicks from the house. All three of us reached the Shadow Hawk at about the same time and quickly clamored into the plane.

"Direct hit sir, if I do say so myself," Alex boasted proudly with a cocky grin as he continued gripping his cannon as if he might need to fire again any second.

"I saw, good shot kid. Pilot! Full throttle towards where that jet crashed!" I shouted.

We got to the crash site to find both of the men standing with their hands raised and trembling in terror, a bullet hole in the ground less than an inch from the taller one's head. After we loaded them onto the Shadow

Hawk, I stepped outside and, using a pair of high power binoculars, looked at the ridge where Jasmine was supposed to be. She was laying there, her rifle next to her, looking through her own pair of high power binoculars with her hand up in the air, thumbs up. I stuck my hand up in the thumbs up sign as well and she put her hand down before lighting a green flare so the pilot could find her. After I quickly put a pair of plasma cuffs on both of the two prisoners and quickly mirandarized them, I pulled them into the Shadow Hawk and had the boys follow me in before we took off and picked up Jasmine from the ridge before turning to return to the base to interrogate the two ex-soldiers. Jasmine and Alex were both beaming with pride and argued the entire way back to the base over who played a more important role in the success of the mission. I hoped that these people could not only help end this twenty year war once and for all, but also help me finally get my revenge on the man who had caused my wife's death. If I could avenge Elana, maybe I could move on and find someone new.

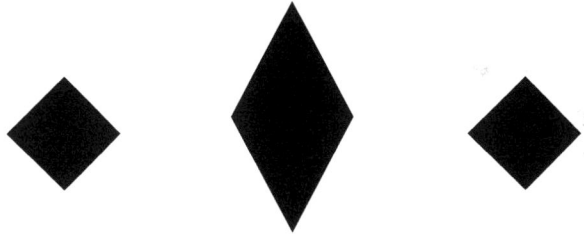

◆ ◆ ◆

When we got back to base, we put each man in separate interrogation chambers, which were plain, small white rooms with energy fields that served as the only way in or out. In the middle of each of the rooms was a small table with a bench on either side. In order to keep the prisoners from using the table or benches as weapons, everything in the room was bolted to the floor of the rooms. According to the records, the men's names were Ray Moon and Michael Wolfe. We were going to interrogate Michael first since he was lower in ranks than Ray.

"Alright," I said as I moved through the field into the room and sat down on the empty bench across the table from Michael, crossing my arms over my chest and glaring into his beady, shifty eyes that were bouncing all around the room, looking at anywhere but back at me. "Let's make this easy for all of us. Just tell us everything you know about King Gary Van' burke and where he might be. Now keep in mind that I am a very impatient man, so if you send us on a wild goose chase and we don't find anything, I promise you, I will come back and slowly cut each and every one of your fingers and toes off nice and slow and ask you again. And if you send us off on another wild goose chase, then I will cut off more and more of you until you are nothing, but a body and a head."

"I-I don't remember where the king said he hid." Michael said in a shaky voice, starting to sweat all over as his eyes moved around the room again even faster.

"Well think hard or I start cutting," I said in a cold, steely voice as I drew a knife from my boot and pretended to look the blade over, making sure he saw that the blade was razor sharp.

"OK, OK, he-he said that it was somewhere in the Andromeda Galaxy. I don't know exactly where. Please, don't hurt me. I have a family. I've changed, and I've just started to get my life turned around," he pleaded as he started to sob and shake uncontrollably, gripping the back of his chair.

"Fine," I said. "I'll leave you to think for a bit while I interrogate your friend."

As I walked out of the interrogation room, I realized that my squad had been watching my interrogation. As they began to walk towards me, I tried to look natural.

"Sir!" Jasmine shouted, running after me. "Sir! Why did you act like that? That won't make him more cooperative! It will scare him into forgetting anything useful. Don't you walk away from me when I am talking to you! Why is this stupid king so important to you anyway!?"

I wheeled around on the spot and glared into her eyes and I saw her tense up and turn pale in sheer terror. She had never seen this side of me, but that was because she never had to. But she had crossed the line.

"Look here you!" I said with a snarl. "Why this king is so important to me is none of your concern. Stay out of my way and things that you are too young to understand. This is personal business."

Then my worst nightmare walked out from between Max and Alex: one of the Control board members.

"Jack." he said in a low tone. "We know how you are involved in this mission, and we think that you are too close to this and need to take a break. The board has already agreed. You are suspended from this case until the interrogation portion is over. You are not allowed to talk to or make any kind of contact with either of the prisoners or your squad until the interrogation portion is over or you will be permanently removed from the armed forces in general. You are allowed to do anything else as long as it doesn't involve this part of the case. Understood?" He finished.

"Yeah, fine. Whatever," I huffed. I had different things on my mind. I walked away and I heard them begin to discuss who was going to interrogate the prisoners now. I had a feeling that they were going to choose Jasmine.

The next day I got up some time before sunrise, went to my private hanger, hopped on my Shadow Cobra, which was my custom motorcycle that I had built from spare parts I had found in a dumpster, turned it on, opened the doors, and drove off away from the base. I was focused on finding the nearby town of Jean, Nevada, and the military cemetery that was in the center of town. As I entered the town, I slowed down to say hello to some of the townspeople who still remembered me, like the gunsmith and the gym owner. As I caught sight of the cemetery, I slowed down and parked my bike against the gates around the outside. I walked in, said hello to the cemetery guard, and kept walking until I got to a tombstone that had two revolvers crossing each other on the top. As I read the inscription, I felt a tear running down my cheek and I quickly wiped it away and looked around to see if anybody had noticed. Once I made sure no one was around, I read the inscription again, out loud this time:

"Elana Marr, a great friend, soldier, and wife that was taken before her time. She will always live on in our hearts as a symbol of friendship, fairness, and the type of true love that never dies." Then, since no one was there to see, I fell on my knees and cried more then I can ever remember crying before. I cried until I couldn't cry anymore. Then I stood up slowly, wiped the tears off my face, straightened up my shirt, brushed the dirt off my knees and elbows, and made my way back to my bike and back to base. I had one more place to visit before I destroyed every single target in the target room. When I got back to the base, I went in and went to the morgue. The morgue was where they put the bodies of the Medal of Honor winners, even though they had a tombstone in the cemetery. I went to the E section and opened up Elana's box just enough so that her head was visible. I bent down and kissed her lips. They were cold and dry, but it still felt good and filled me with loving warmth that I hadn't felt in three years. Then I slid the box closed and slowly made my way out of the morgue and to the target room.

Chapter 8

About a week later, I finally got word that the others had cracked the retired guards and gotten some information out of them, which meant I could meet with my squad. I made my way down the hallway to the interrogation wing so that I could finally hear what the guards had said.

"Alright," I said as I entered the conference chamber. "What did they say? What did you get out of them?"

"He said that it was on Planet Xenon in the Andromeda Galaxy," Jasmine said in a low tone.

"OK," I said. I turned around to face a private that I had heard walk by on his way to the control bridge

"Private, when you get to the control bridge, tell one of them to run a surface scan of Planet Xenon for any large objects with lots of life forms inside it."

"Yes, sir," the private said before hurrying off to the control bridge.

"What did you do with the retired guards after you interrogated them? Do you still have them?" I asked.

"No, we sent them back to their worlds, neither of which was even in the Andromeda Galaxy."

I couldn't believe that they had just let them go, even if neither of the guards were in the same galaxy as the king was supposedly in.

"Sir," the private I had sent up the bridge said when he returned. "Our scanners have detected a large object on the surface of the Planet

Xenon with several thousand life forms in it and in the thirty mile perimeter around it, sir."

"Thank you private. That is all for now," I said.

The private then ran off to attend to other duties as I turned to face my squad.

"Alright, we have our next mission. This will be very different for you since it will be your first time on another planet, and your first time in another galaxy. We will be taking the base since we will need a lot of backup if there are as many life forms as that private said there was." I told the cadets.

"What? We're taking the base? What do you mean? The base turns into a tank, not a spaceship," Max interrupted.

"Correction," I said. "It can turn into both a tank and a spaceship."

"Wow," they all said in unison with a shocked look in their eyes.

"We will be leaving in three days for Planet Xenon. It will take another three days to get there. We will send a scout squad ahead to see what we are up against. I'm not sure we should do that, but I lost most of my control when I got suspended!" I said with a glare at Jasmine.

"Sorry, I didn't mean to get you suspended, but I was just upset about how you had treated him," Jasmine said softly.

Alex lay his arm around her shoulder and shot a glare back at me.

"Jasmine took it really hard. You shouldn't have been so hard on her. She didn't know how personal this was to you. She just wanted to be nice," Max said in the same soft tone.

I felt slightly bad about upsetting Jasmine, but she had pushed my buttons. I walked out the door towards the arsenal room to prepare my guns for the trip to the Andromeda Galaxy.

Chapter 9

Three days later, it was time for the trip to Xenon. All of the troops in the base were rushing around to make some quick last minute adjustments for the flight. When we were all set to go, I made my way to the control center. I had to be there to authorize the transformation. When I got to the control center, one of the engineers was using the intercom to clear the last of the hallways. If anyone was in the hallways during the transformation, they would be crushed by the walls as they moved to transform the base into a large, powerful shuttle. I knew exactly how it looked, because I had been caught in it once, but that was another story.

"Alright, are all the hallways cleared?" I asked.

"Yes, sir. We are clear for transformation process. We just need your authorization," the engineer confirmed.

"Right, I haven't turned this thing into a shuttle in three years." I stated as I walked up and sat down in the chair in front of the control panel. I put my hand on a hand print on the screen to authorize the transformation. I grinned broadly as the control room turned upward towards the sky. I heard a few more parts snap into place. When that was done, the screen said that the transformation had been completed.

"Thank goodness nothing went wrong this time," I said with a sigh of relief.

"Alright, time to put get this bird in the air. Engage launch check list. Check primary fuel tanks and landing gear, as well as the reentry shield and the primary and auxiliary thrusters. Then engage the space gear shelves," I called to the engineers in the control center.

A few minutes later, the engineers had completed the primary and secondary launch checklists and we were ready for takeoff. Most of the troops on the ship would probably pass out from the G-forces and I would have to pilot the ship into a gentle, calm orbit around the Earth until most of the engineers had woken up.

"Final system checks complete sir," one of the engineers said.

"Engage primary thrusters." I said. I heard a rumble, and we were taking off.

"There we go. Engage auxiliary thrusters, now," I said.

I heard a second rumble, and I looked out the window to see the sky begin to darken as we left Earth's atmosphere. I felt the rush of G-forces, heard all of the engineers pass out, took control of the steering wheel, and began to pilot the shuttle into a steady orbit around the earth. Once I got everything under control, I realized that I still had to put my suit on. I pressed the autopilot button, released the harness that was keeping me strapped to my seat, and floated out the bridge and towards the nearest rack of space suits. I realized how quiet the ship was since all the troops on the ship had passed out from the G-forces. The only sound to be heard was the sound of me zipping up the suit and fastening on a helmet. After that was done, I engaged my gravity boots and made my way to the shooting range, which was coincidentally the only place with automatic artificial gravity. All the other places had a button in the control center with their names on them that engaged the artificial gravity. As I reached the door to the shooting range, I heard the engines reactivate to send us to our next destination: Planet Xenon, Andromeda galaxy. *"And the king's final resting place,"* I thought hopefully to myself.

Chapter 10

Almost two weeks later, we arrived twenty miles from the large object on the Planet Xenon's surface that was supposedly the king's fortress. I was shaking with anticipation while I checked and rechecked my weapons. We had sent a scout squad out when we had arrived an hour ago and still hadn't heard from them. Finally, I heard the intercom tone and a voice urgently requesting me to report to the control center immediately. I ran up to the control center, nearly running over a group of privates walking to lunch in perfect formation. When I skidded into the control center, I knew at once why I had been called there. The holo-projector in the center of the room had a fuzzy projection of the leader of the scout squad we had sent out earlier with several injuries along his body. He was shouting something but there was horrible reception.

"Boost the receiving signal," I called to the engineers.

One of the engineers turned a dial and the projection became clearer.

"They discovered us…pinned down…Area D13!" The image fizzled and we lost the reception.

"What are we going to do!?" one of the privates asked in a frightened tone.

"Prep the ships. We found them," I said. I was finally going to get revenge on the man who killed my wife. I was coming, and I was out for blood. No exceptions, no survivors.

I walked into the squad's chamber with a dangerous look on my face and watched as their heads turned as soon as I entered the room.

"Listen up, get all your gear on and meet me in the arsenal room ASAP," I said simply, and then left the room.

When the squad walked into the arsenal room a minute later, they had all their armor on aside from their helmets. It was a titanium carbon alloy that was virtually indestructible, but only to a certain extent that also had small gaps in some places. As they walked in, I just couldn't help, but feel like I was seeing a perfect replica of my squad.

"As you know," I said. "Today we will be attempting the greatest attack in history. The casualties will be high, but they will be even higher if we don't try. If any of you want to back out now, I will fully understand and will not blame you at all."

They stood there in perfect formation, not moving a muscle.

"I think I speak for all of us when I say that we've come too far to back down now, sir," Jasmine said bravely, her eyes hard with determination.

"Alright, well, then there is one more thing left to do. Instead of assigning you regular weapons, you will build your own, just like I did when I was your rank," I said.

"What!?" they all shouted in unison.

"You heard me right. You will be making your own weapons," I stated calmly.

When they had finished their personalized weapons, I was glad to see how creative they had been.

"The last thing we need to do before you can take these into battle is name them. I assume you already have ideas, so I'll just ask you one by one. What is the name you have for yours Alex?" I asked.

"The Titan Cannon," Alex said proudly. It was jet black and about three feet long with several fuel canisters attached to the back, and several sets of vents.

"What about yours Jasmine?" I asked.

"The Semper Snipe AS10," said Jasmine. Hers was a color that seemed to be changing in the light. It had a large magazine, a sliding rail with a scope, and several notches on the side, one of which was holding a silencer.

"And what about yours Max?" I asked.

"The Arc Rifle," said Max, his eyes beaming with pride. His seemed slightly small for a rifle, but I knew that it had a rail magazine and a monitor to help him keep track of his ammunition. It had an under mounted grenade launcher with several small gears that seemed to rotate in place.

I noticed they all had a smirk that they were trying to hide.

"Is there something you three aren't telling me?" I asked.

"Yes, there is," they said at the same time.

They bent over and held their guns close together. They pulled back several mechanisms on the top and bottom parts of the guns and the guns snapped together. Alex's cannon made up the center and base, with Jasmine's rifle on the left side, and Max's assault rifle on the right side.

Then, they all gripped a large handle that extended from the backs of the guns and held it up to show me.

"We have one more gun to name," Alex said.

"Well, what do you have in mind?" I asked with a grin.

"The Shadowbringer, that's what we agreed on," Jasmine stated.

"Well, I guess I should start to brief you on our current mission," I said. "If our mission is a success, then we will finally end this war. We will be raiding the castle of an infamous king who is known for being the primary cause of this war. We will be flown in several minutes after the main group of troops has arrived. We know that the palace is heavily guarded and filled with several million troops. You will be using your newly built guns, and there will most likely be air support, so keep an eye on the sky, Alex."

"Yes sir," Alex said with a strong tone in his voice.

"Jasmine, you will be in charge of the snipers on the ship. Your job is to provide covering fire while the troops advance or are dropped off. Do not, under any circumstances, exit the ship until the battle is over, understood?

"Yes sir," said Jasmine, giving a swift nod of her head.

"Max, you will be in charge of the primary infantry force. I will go ahead and help clear a pathway from one trench to another, and then you will move the troops forward after I reach the next barricade, understood?"

"Yes sir," Max said.

"Alright, let's go. Everybody onto the War Falcon."

We went to the hanger, got into the extremely large ship called a War Falcon, and took off.

Chapter 11

As we started to take off, I looked around at all the troops with us in the War Falcon gunship. We had been flying for an hour and a half when I heard bells ringing. Then, I saw Alex, Max, and Jasmine come out of the doors that led to the cargo hold, each holding a small box in their hands.

"Do you want me to check your ammo for you? I already checked it before we left," I said.

"No, we have something to say: Merry Christmas, sir."

I realized with a look at my watch that it was the twenty fifth of December. I had completely forgotten about Christmas. I held out my hands, feeling dumbstruck, to receive my presents. I then opened them one by one. Jasmine had gotten me a necklace with a stone cross on it with two blades going across the middle of it. Max had gotten me a small box that turned out to be a mini transport box. I opened Alex's present last. It was a chip that he told me to put on my sword handle. I put it on and a ray of energy surrounded my sword blades. It was an energy chip. I went to the cargo hold and stored two uranium carbon rod cannons inside the storage box Max had given me and put it on my belt before going back up to the main area to join my squad. We were about to land in drop zone B52, Area D13, the 'D' standing for death.

We were landing a minute later. Everyone was checking their weapons and ammo. Before we had even finish landing, the ship shook. We had been hit. We heard several large bangs that I knew were the ship's cannons returning fire on the enemy artillery guns. When the ship touched down, everybody, except the snipers, ran off the ship just like they had in all the practice dust-offs they had done before.

"Let's go! Move it!" I hollered.

Once all of us had gotten off, the ship rose up into the air with the snipers onboard and moved back to a safer position that was out of reach of the artillery cannons. Alex rallied the other artillery gunners and they all fired at the same time at each of the artillery cannons, destroying each with one set. It helped quite a bit that Alex was using his Titan. Now, all the troops were very heavily loaded down with weapons and ammo, but compared to them, I was a walking arsenal. I had two waist holders and two ankle holsters that contained .75 caliber Jungle Hawk pistols, as well as a shotgun, a light machine gun, and a Gatling turret of my own making strapped to my back, and my blood pistol was tucked away in its holster in the small of my back with an engraved bullet that had a simple message on it: Screw U!

"Ready?" I asked Max. He simply nodded.

"Alright, three, two, one, GO!" I shouted and all of the infantry men behind us began to provide me covering fire, and I stormed out of the trench. It didn't matter how much they fired. I had to do most of the work. I pulled out the light machine gun and began to fire. The enemy troops were storming out of a large door on a huge barricade that I assumed was surrounding the palace. They were charging at me, but they couldn't seem to hit me. Bullets whizzed past my face as I cut them down row by row, but they kept coming. I kept shooting. The memory of my wife dying in my arms blinded me with rage. My light machine gun ran out of ammo, so I threw it at some of the alien foot soldiers, knocking them off their feet. A couple more of the enemy troops behind them tripped over their fallen comrades. I pulled out my Gatling turret and began to fire once more. They must have guessed that we were coming because they already had snipers and cannons set up on top of the barricade. The cannons had my troops trapped and I saw a squad of enemy troops headed towards their trench. I shot the troops, then turned around and put my Gatling turret away to face the barricade, and tapped the release button on the side of my storage unit on my belt. Two enormous H43 duo-laser cannons materialized on my shoulders. The H43 cannon was one of a series of weapons based off of a design originally created by my father that utilized both a carbon dioxide laser and a neodymium laser with several different firing capabilities, one of which I had designed myself. The cannon was designed to be able to fire either the carbon dioxide laser or the neodymium laser on its own as either a concentrated laser beam or as a concentrated shot of energy that resembles a shoulder-mounted rocket or to fire a energy shot of both lasers at the same time, and my modifications provide a new feature that was only for worst case scenarios since it drained the entire battery in one pull of the trigger, whereas the original firing formats got five shots out of a battery. I looked down the two precision self-calibrating electronic scopes on the cannons, locked on to one of the turrets and fired. For an instant the entire battlefield seemed to go silent, as if all of the troops on both sides had stopped to stare at the two large beams of energy consisting of both lasers heading towards the cannon. Then, they hit the cannon and the whole thing exploded into a large bright blast of energy. I quickly turned and fired again at the next one, again and again until I had destroyed all four cannons on this side of the wall surrounding the palace. Finally, with one shot left in the dual-energy battery tubes I had loaded into each cannon, I locked my sights on the huge part of the wall where the door had closed. I fired and there was a large blast, but the doors didn't break, they just dented slightly. I dropped down into cover of the trench that my teammates were in and reloaded the cannons. I stood back up and held the trigger down. The four beam generators began to spin around in a circle and glow a bright purple. They kept spinning, and when I heard a small tone that meant it was about to go into overload, I released the trigger. Both cannons shot a blinding spiral-shaped beam of energy. In case you're wondering, yes, that was my modified firing mode. Upon hitting the door, there was a rippling concussive wave, the sound of the deafening explosion only following after a few milliseconds of what felt like silence caused by the eardrum-smashing effect of the concussive wave. The door and the part of the barricade above it were completely obliterated by the explosion. After a soft hissing emitted from the cannons, the two empty battery tubes shot out of the exit port and I put the cannons away. A second later a huge swarm of troops and aircrafts swarmed out of the hole in the barricade to protect the palace. I heard a cannon fire and looked up just in time to see a green ball of energy that was unmistakably fired from the Titan fly up and destroy an enemy jet that was approaching our position.

"Max, stay here and watch for other attacks. Do not follow me into the palace. Just help me clear a path. Do I make myself clear?" I asked.

I saw a look of longing in his eyes, but a second later it was gone.

"Yes sir," he said. "And sir?" He turned to face me, staring into my eyes. "Kick some ass in there." A wild maniac grin lit up his face.

I nodded to him before running forward, firing my Gatling gun everywhere and cutting a hole through the wave of enemies. My Gatling gun ran out of ammo almost as soon as I got past the primary defenses. I put it on my back with my light machine gun that I had found in the charge, pulled out two of my Jungle Hawk pistols, and began making my way to the doors of the palace. I was about to open the doors when a large group of enemy troops tried to charge me from behind. It took all of my ammo from all four of my pistols to finish them all, but I was about to get my revenge. It was worth it.

Chapter 12

I made my way towards the top floor of the palace where, according to the recon information we got before we left earth, was where the king was supposed to be. As I made my way up the third flight of stairs, I ran straight into a guard. Before he could say a word, I had pulled out my dagger and pierced his throat. I left him there, the dagger still in his throat. I didn't have time to hide the body and all that junk. A few floors later, I came to a corner, flattened myself against the wall, and looked around. I soon spotted a guard staring out the window onto the battlefield. I snuck up behind him with my blood pistol, locked the blades, and dragged them across his throat. I left him there as well. Another four floors, I ran into half a squad of guards. I pulled out my sword with the energy blade on it. Before they even had a chance to draw their guns, I had killed each one of them with one slice each. About a minute later, I had finally made it to the king's chamber.

As I smashed through the door into the king's chamber, I pulled out my blood pistol with that single engraved bullet. Suddenly, the king began to smile.

"What's so funny?" I asked.

The truth hit me as the sound of at least twenty guards storming into the room. They filed into the room with full auto machine guns and surrounded me.

"Oh shit," I swore under my breath.

The king was revolting to look at. He belonged to an alien race known as *Laminis Fodiente Peregrínus*, and nicknamed 'Sawheads.' This nickname came from the fact that running down the center of the alien's sickly pale green face was a bone blade the ran from just under the creature's chin, up over the face, and ended in a point just above their forehead. Their faces were symmetrical on either side of the blade. On each side there were two crimson red eyes with black pupils and one mouth on either side that was full of serrated, needle sharp teeth and were constantly dripping saliva. These two separate mouths resulted in the species having two separate voices. One voice was a deep bass voice and the other was a high pitched screechy voice, resulting in the fact that it was very hard to understand.

"Kill him. Kill him now!" the king screeched furiously with his two-tone voice.

The guards fired at me simultaneously and I fell to the ground in more pain than I had never felt before in my life. However, I soon heard the king scream in pain. Apparently a stray bullet from the guard behind me hit him in the eye, which did make me feel a bit better. The king ordered for the guard who shot him and I to be thrown off the ship since it was already taking off. As I hit the ground, the last thing I remember before I blacked out was someone running towards me, calling my name and calling for a medic. Then, I let a cold darkness overcome my vision, and died.

Chapter 13

Everything went black and I saw a small, far away looking white light. I thought that I might be able to come back if I go through it, then thought of all the movies I had seen where the dead person saw a light and went towards it and completely died. Before I could make a decision, the white light suddenly zoomed towards me and engulfed me. When I opened my eyes, I saw that it looked like I was standing on a gray smoke of some kind. Then I heard a growl and looked up to see two giants coming towards me with clubs the size of a bus. I pulled out my shotgun, but it turned to dust in my hands. I tried to pull out my pistols and then my Gatling gun, but they all turned to dust as well as soon as my hands touched them.

"Come on!" I shouted, raising my hands in exasperation.

The giants were getting closer and closer, and then I remembered my swords and blades. I pulled out my sword, and it turned to dust. Then I pulled out the pair of blades I had hidden in a leather strap under my sleeves. They didn't turn to dust, so I jumped up and stood right behind one of the giant's heads, but right before the blade touches his skin, it turned to dust. I tried to think of what to do as the giant tried to grab me. Finally, I wrapped my arms around his giant neck and barely made my arms connect. So I grabbed one hand with the other and pulled. The giant tried to shake me off before he crashed down to the floor and turned to dust the way my weapons had. I had almost forgotten that there were two giants until I saw a giant foot shadow over me. I looked up to see that the giant was right on top of me. I looked away and expected to be crushed, but it never happened. I heard a rush of wind and the shadow moved away from me. I looked and saw the giant crash to the floor and disintegrate. Then, I saw who had saved me and nearly passed out. It was Elana, my dead wife.

"Jack!" she cried.

"Elana?!" I said in shock.

We ran together and collided into a hug. For a second I didn't care that I was dead. I had my wife back. She was still four inches shorter than me at six feet two, and her golden blonde hair and sparkling green eyes were as beautiful as ever. She didn't even look like she had aged since her death at forty-three years old.

"Oh Jack, I missed you so much. But I need to take you to Him," she said.

"Who?" I asked.

"Him. I don't know who He is but He's in charge," she said.

"Alright, I love surprises," I said.

We walked towards a large white pair of doors and when Elana touched the doors, they swung open to reveal a large throne room. There was an old man that was at least twice the size of the giants sitting in a large throne.

"Jack Maxus Marr." He boomed in a low tone.

"That's me," I said.

"You have finally joined us here."

"Yeah, about that, I need to go back," I said nervously, rubbing the back of my neck.

"What!?" The old man and Elana both asked simultaneously.

"I need to go back and save the universe from an evil tyrant. I need to help my squad," I replied.

"Once you come here, there is no going back," He said flatly.

"I know, but don't you want to have your creations thrive? If I don't go back, everything will be destroyed," I pleaded.

"I cannot let…" He started.

"I don't care. If you don't let me back now, I will destroy this place finding my own way back. That I can promise you," I interrupted. I noticed that Elana looked nervously at me, then at Him, and then back to me again.

"Fine, you have proven your point. I will allow you to go back. Not only that, but I shall make it so that you will never age. You can still be injured, mind you, but time will have no effect on you," He said.

"Also, could I bring Elana with me?" I asked. "Ever since I lost her, I have never been able to focus on anything else. I turned into a mean, old man that is famous for how badly he treats people. I've lost my edge. I have never been able to make another perfect score on anything."

He sighed deeply for a moment, and then looked back at us.

"Fine, you will have what you requested. And she shall also be untouched by time, just like you. This will allow you all to continue to protect and serve the galaxy. But this results in one condition. As soon as you spawn an heir to your role as protector and your heir comes of age to do his job, the time elapsed between your death and resurrection will return to you at once." He said to both me and Elana.

"Thank you so much, and I agree to the condition." I said happily. Then I turned and saw Elana start to cry. I knew they were tears of happiness and I felt tears welling up in my eyes, and I didn't even care when I felt them running down my cheek. We ran together and she kissed me, and it felt even better than ever before. Then there was a flash of light and I woke up on a hospital bed, with my squad standing around me.

"Hey guys, what's up?" I said.

Chapter 14

For a second, everybody just stood there staring at me. Max was the first to speak.

"Are you a zombie?" he asked.

"I haven't been dead that long. Just call it a medical miracle. Oh shit, I forgot! Move!" I said as I bolted out the room. I didn't care that I was only wearing a hospital gown. I ran straight through to the morgue. I ran straight to the E section and heard the banging sound coming from the inside of one of the boxes. I opened it up and Elana shot up so fast that she nearly hit her head. I gave her my gown and told her to go out and get me another gown. When she got back, she handed me the gown and I slipped it on. Then we went back to the doors together and made our way to the hospital wing of the base. The whole way back we had to put up with troop after troop saluting nervously. When we finally made it back to the hospital wing, my squad took one look at Elana and I knew that I had some explaining to do.

"Alright everybody, first of all, I am not a zombie. I am a person who had a conversation with a spiritual being and came back to life. Second, this is not a spy or a thief or someone who had broken in. This is Elana, Elana Marr," I explained slowly,

They all gasped and looked back and forth between me and Elana, then back at me.

"So, she's your little sister?" Jasmine asked.

"No. What? No, she's my wife," I replied.

"Yes, you must be Max, Alex, and Jasmine," Elana said sweetly.

"Yep, I'm Alex, nice to meet you," Alex said.

"I'm Jason, but I prefer Max. You look nice," Max said, and then whimpered slightly from a look from me.

Elana shook the guys' hands, and then shook Jasmine's.

"Well, I'm glad that we have all met," I said. "Now, I have a few questions for Elana. First of all, when do you want to go back to work, and second, will you be working at the base or in the field?"

"Always work first with you Jack. I guess I'll start tomorrow in the field. I was hoping I could work in your squad, if that's ok with you," replied my wife.

"Sure. That'd be great," I said. I was so glad that I could hardly contain it.

"If you want, you can sleep with me in my room," Max said.

I took Max off to the side for a second.

"Before you go on talking to MY wife, I want to show you something." I pulled out my blood pistol and showed it to him. "I forged these blades myself by hand in the fires of Mt. Lay off My Wife!" I said with a glare.

Chapter 15

When we had all decided on where Elana would sleep (my room) and when we were going to go back to work (tomorrow), we went back to our rooms and slept. The next day, we woke up and went to the war room.

"Alright, I want to hear every single thing that happened between when I died and when I came back to life," I declared.

"Well, after we got to your body," Jasmine said, "Alex fired several times at the palace that turned out to be a large space ship. He also fired a small flashing projectile. I saw it hit the ship, but it never exploded, so I asked him what it was, and he said that it was a tracking beacon."

"So now, with the help of some of the engineers here, I have locked on the beacon's signal and they appear to have landed about two light years away on the planet Jaxom V," continued Alex. "And we were about to put your body in the morgue when you woke up."

"Well, let's go!" I said. I started to run towards the door when I suddenly felt a stabbing pain shoot up through my leg and felt it buckle.

"Jack? Are you ok?" Elana asked as she ran to help me to my feet.

"Yeah, I'm fine. Don't worry. I guess I'm still sore from when I died. Man that sounded weird," I commented as I stood back up.

"I guess we're going to have to wait on the attack, at least until you are back in shape and battle-ready," Elana said.

"Fine, but we should still go, so that we can scope out the area. Everyone prep for takeoff. We're going to Jaxom V."

"Sweet, we're going back into space!" Max said, punching a fist in the air.

"Alright, let's roll. Everyone go to the arsenal room and prep your guns for space travel. I'm going to train you so hard you might want to throw yourselves out the airlock," I said with a grin.

"You mind setting my guns up for the travel for me? I have to go and authorize the launch and transformation," I asked Elana.

"Sure, I'll do it. You still have my guns?" she asked me.

"Yeah, I never got rid of them. They're in our personal arsenal area," I answered with a grin.

Elana went out one door and I went out the other door to the control center to engage the transformation.

◆ ◆ ◆

Once we were in space, and the kids and Elana had regained consciousness, we went down to the arsenal room and started what was definitely the most grueling training set I had ever done. I went off if the bullets was even half an inch to the side of the bull's-eye or if there was a single piece of ship left after Alex fired at his target. The only thing that seemed to keep them from going nuts was Elana, who was always there to support them or cheer them up after one of my complaints. I kept telling her that babying them wouldn't help them fight better. I just want them to survive. Then one day, she snapped.

"Look Jack. I know what you want. You don't just want them to survive. You want them to be you!" she shouted and then stormed off out of the room.

Chapter 16

A week and a half later, we finally made it to Jaxom V. Elana was still mad at me even though I had tried to be nicer to the kids. Our unmanned spy plane (my alternative to a scout squad) had given us all the information we needed to plan the attack. We were about to load up the jets, we had to do it early in the morning to avoid the desert heat of the day on this planet, when I heard someone say something.

"Hey! You were leaving without me?" Elana asked from somewhere behind me.

"No, we thought you might want to leave with the second group so that you didn't have to be up so early," I said, turning around to face her.

"No, you wanted to leave without me. I'm going with you and your squad, and I'm going now," she said matter-of-factly.

"Fine, get in," I said. I didn't even try to argue with her and if you ever meet her, I recommend that you take my advice and do the same. We got into the Death Falcon and were on the way to finally end this war. While we were sitting in the cargo area prepping our guns, a scout pilot radioed in and told us that the base was heavily loaded with several artillery guns and turrets set up all over the perimeter of the ship/palace.

"Did you hear that Alex? Get five hundred charges off the ammo wall and I'll brief you on my newest plan. We are going to use the element of surprise to our advantage. We can use these charges, thank you Alex, to destroy all the turrets and cannons so that they can't use them. Last time we split up, I died. So instead, this time we stick together, at least until we get to the ship/palace. Alex, when we get to the palace I want you to go around the perimeter of the ship and place charges against where the ground meets the ship. That way if the ship tries to take off, you can just detonate the charges, and the ship will be unable to take off. It can't fly with broken engines right?" I asked with a chuckle. We all laughed a little. Jokes were good for breaking the tension. I remember that my old commander had always said that the tension was what kept us alive. "Anyways, Jasmine, I want you to look out the windows as we go up through the ship. Snipe the enemies that our troops can't get to. Max, you stick with me and Elana and provide extra support, but try to stay hidden. If we can, I want to get to the king's chamber without being spotted if possible. That's why we're attacking so early. That and because it's burning hot as soon as the sun comes up, but mostly to stay hidden. That's also what most of the charges are for. We are going to sneak up to the cannons and put a single charge on each cannon. We don't need more than one on each cannon. Elana, you stick with me and we'll have no problem getting in one way or another. Just like last time though, Alex, we have information that they have gunships. Just in time, we're landing, everybody off as quietly as possible."

Chapter 17

We all filed off the ship and Alex passed out the charges to the five hundred troops in front of us. Once everybody had a charge, I told them how it was going to work.

"Listen up everyone," I whispered, "we all need to be completely silent. Once you've placed your charge, meet back here and wait for further orders. Ready? We only get one shot at this, but if we do it right, we can finally end this war forever, so let's go." I finished and we all scattered off towards the cannons. Some of the stronger troops, including Alex and Max, and I scaled the wall and put charges on the large cannons at the top. Then, we all got back to the ship, loaded up our guns, got into the ship, and when everyone was in the ship, I flipped the switch. There was a loud series of explosions and we felt the ground tremble. We knew that the plan had worked. We all charged out of the ship and started firing. The few enemy scouts that were still on the wall were quickly gunned down. We charged out as the large door in the wall opened and the enemies started pouring out. We pushed through with everyone covering Alex, ducking every time he fired at an enemy jet. We were soon able to get through the door just in time before it closed. Alex put his cannon in his storage unit that I had bought him, pulled out his M25A9 assault rifle, and chambered the round. As we began to move forward, I pulled out my sword and Elana pulled out her knife. We crept into the ship as Alex broke off to place the remaining charges around the outside. We silently made our way through the ship and after running into several groups of guards, finally made it to the top floor. We waited for Alex and once he arrived, we prepped to breach the door. We were quickly able to blast open the door, leading us to find an empty throne room. There was an opening in the ceiling that I knew he must have climbed through to escape.

"No way is he escaping me again!" I shouted as I jumped up to get to the hatch.

I pulled myself up, killed the two guards and pointed my blood pistol at the king as he sat there quivering in fear.

"Remember me? The man you killed about a week ago? Well I'm back!" I hollered.

"Jack, stop." I heard. I twirled around, still pointing my blood pistol at the king to see Elana pulling herself through the hatch.

"Why? Why shouldn't I kill this monster? Give me one good reason," I asked coldly.

"You shouldn't kill him because if you do, you'll be no better than him," she said defiantly.

It was like being shot again. It hit me hard in the chest and knocked the wind right out of me.

"How could you compare me to this monster? He killed us. He separated us for three long years," I said with a gasp.

"Just put the gun down," she said calmingly, like she was a police officer talking to a robber.

"Why would letting him live be better then killing him here and now?" I asked.

"Because if you don't kill him now, I will make sure he spends the rest of his life in galactic prison. I may have been dead for five years, but I'm sure they'll remember me. Now put the gun down Jack," she said.

I slowly lowered my gun and put it back in my holster. I grabbed the king by the scruff of his neck, which was covered in sweat, and brought him to the opening in the floor. I dropped him and he hit the ground with a thud.

"Jack!" Elana started.

"Don't worry, he's not dead, just out cold," I said with a smirk, jumping back down to the throne room before helping Elana down.

"Who is this guy, sir?" Jasmine asked, taking a closer look at the unconscious king.

"His name is King Gary Van 'burke," I answered, "and call me Jack."

Chapter 18

The next few days after we returned to Earth were some of the best days of my life. Two days after we got back to Earth, Alex called us down to the mess hall for what he said was an important announcement.

"As you know," he started nervously, "I have called you here for an important announcement. Jasmine, can you come here for a moment?"

Jasmine walked up to him and when she was standing right in front of him, he pulled out a small black box, got down on one knee, and as he opened the box he asked:

"Jasmine, will you marry me?"

"Yes, of course I will!" she shrieked with a leap of joy. Then she slipped on the beautiful diamond ring I had helped him make as everybody applauded for the new couple.

♦ ♦ ♦

Three days later, it was time for the wedding. Elana and I also decided to renew our vows after Jasmine's and Alex's wedding. I had picked out a nice tux for Alex but Elana wouldn't let anybody but herself and Jasmine see Jasmine's dress. Elana and I had decided to don our old wedding clothes, which I was surprised to see still fit me, and we were going to have it in a wide open field overlooking an ocean view that men had rumored to have killed for. It was a picture perfect day. The sun was just beginning to set as the wedding started and there wasn't a single cloud in the sky. We had gathered what we could find of Alex's friend since, like me, he didn't know his parents or family, and Jasmine's parents, three cousins, two sisters, and older brother. The priest was a friend of mine who I had saved and had done my wedding with Elana many years ago. The cake was one I had had made in town by another good friend. I didn't really pay attention to the stuff the priest said about loving each other no matter what happened because I had already heard it all before. I couldn't help marveling at how beautiful Jasmine and Elana looked in their wedding dresses. Elana's was a simple strapless dress that was pure as fresh snow and had small clear diamonds running down the sides and back. Jasmine's was much larger and trailed behind her. Her dress was covered in sparkling pink diamonds and caught the sunlight perfectly on the altar. When Alex and Jasmine sealed the deal with the wedding kiss and after our ceremony, we cut the cake and partied late into the night. I felt better than I could ever remember feeling in my life. Not just for me, but for the new couple.

  After most of the other people had left, Elana and I sat on the edge of the cliff and dangled our feet over the edge.

  "Sometimes I wish that things could just stay peaceful and happy, you know what I mean?" I asked Elana.

  "Well, you know, there is one way that you can make that happen. You've served more than enough years to retire. It just takes one phone call to the board," Elana insisted softly.

  "Yeah, but remember our deal with Him? We get to stay if we keep the universe safe. And know that I know that there is someone up there controlling everything, I want to make sure that I stay on his good side, if you know what I mean." I chuckled.

"Yeah, I know what you mean." She said with a soft chuckle of her own.

I went to bed that night with a smile that nobody could remember ever seeing on me before. There was no way I could have known that the joy I felt that night could only last so long before I was forced to face cold harsh reality again.

Part Two: A Shadow from The Past

Chapter 19

That cold, harsh reality came as a seemingly innocent phone call in the middle of the night about three weeks after the wedding. When I answered it I thought that it was just the press calling for another interview about bringing down the king again. Boy was I wrong.

"Hello? Why are you stupid reporters always calling in the middle of the night? Do you think it helps you get better results or something?" I asked, stifling a yawn.

"Hello Jack, it's been too long. How's Elana?" asked a low droning voice.

"What! How did you find us? How are you alive?" I said, fighting to keep my voice down to a whisper to keep from waking up Elana as my still sleepy brain struggled to try and put the details of the voice I was hearing on the phone together to with a reasonable explanation that would fit, but nothing did. Except for one, the one that I kept wishing couldn't be true.

"It's good to see you too," the voice said with a soft deep chuckle.

"This can't be happening," I thought over and over again, *"There is no way he's alive. I saw him executed. He's dead. I know he's dead."*

"Look, whoever you are, this isn't funny," I growled as I tried to sound intimidating without raising my voice.

"This isn't a joke Jack, and you know that. Well, I've got to go now, but I can't wait to see you and Elana again."

I slammed the phone down on the receiver and went back to bed, but I couldn't sleep. I kept telling myself that this couldn't be happening.

It was just someone playing a trick on me. It didn't help. I knew it wasn't a joke. He was back, and it was my job to stop him again, just like last time.

      The next day Elana and I took a shuttle from my private Villa in Rome to the nearest international airport. Then from there we took a direct flight to Jean in Nevada back in the US. I told her the details of the call last night and it was everything she could do to keep from shouting and panicking on the airplane. Then from our house in Jean, I took my custom Ferrari and drove out to Constellation Division's base, which is located two lefts and a right from the middle of nowhere and is the home base of my team. Once we got to my underground private garage and parked the car, we took the elevator straight up to the control center. We set it to direct route so that it wouldn't make any stops along the way. Once the doors opened I burst through with Elana right behind me.

      "Hello sir," one of the technicians began.

      "We have a problem. He's back. Mario is back," I said quickly, cutting him off and making every head in the control room turn quickly to look at Elana and myself. Everybody knew who Mario was, even though it had been fifteen years since anybody had heard of him, but Mario was a name that nobody in the service was likely to forget for some time.

      "That's right. He called me last night at my Villa. He said he's back and he's looking for me. He said he can't wait to see me again." I said.

      "We'll call the rest of your squad and get to work right…" The technician started.

      "No!" I cut him off again. "You can call Max but leave Jasmine and Alex out of this until they finish their honeymoon in Vegas. I don't want them to end up like me and Elana." That's right, after the wedding, Alex and Jasmine had taken off on their honeymoon, and they chose

Vegas for obvious reasons. Max was the only other member of the team that wasn't preoccupied, and he was also ironically the only remaining member of Shadowstar Squad who wasn't married or even in a relationship, but maybe that was a good thing. Anyways, I figured that when everyone else had taken off for vacation after the wedding that Max would have as well. Unbeknownst to me, Max was actually much closer than I had originally thought. I told them to call up Max ASAP and went down to the private hanger again to get the few small suitcases that we had brought from Rome to bring them up to our room.

Chapter 20

I was coming back from the garage carrying our luggage from the car to our old room when I heard a voice somewhere on the other side of the pile of luggage I was carrying.

"Hey Jack, let me help you with that," it said.

I figured it was just a cadet who was bored and walking around instead of being in class.

"First of all, I've got it, second, why aren't you in class, and third, you should already know how to correctly address a higher officer."

"Well then, first of all, ok, second, I don't need to be in class for another hour, and third, I'm just calling you what you told me to call you."

I recognized it all at the same time. The tone, the attitude, it all came back.

"Max!" I said. "What's up man? What are you doing here and what do you mean when you said that you didn't have class for another hour?"

"I mean that I'm a teacher. I got the promotion a few days ago. I'm teaching how to fix a jam and how to clean the weapons."

"How ironic," I chuckled. "I mean you were the one who was freaking out because he forgot to chamber the first round!"

"Yeah, those were some good times. So what brings you here? Last I heard you were relaxing in your private villa in Rome."

"So they haven't told you about him yet." I mumbled, more to myself then to Max.

"They haven't told me about whom?" Max asked "Is it that King guy? Has he escaped?"

"No, Van'burke is locked in the middle of an asteroid. He's never getting out," I said.

"Then what is it? Tell me how I can help," Max said. He was as stubborn as ever.

"Fine, I'll call in a sub for your class. This could take a while," I said.

"No, no sub can handle my five P.M. class. I've tried every sub in the United States and half of them went mad after ten minutes," Max said.

"You see, that's what you did wrong. You tried to use American subs. You need the best. You need a Russian sub. And I know just the guy. His name is Victor Caesar. Trust me. He was my sub and he kept me in line for sure. So if he can handle me, he can handle any group of kids."

"I don't know," Max said. "I mean these kids are horrible. I have trouble just keeping them under control enough to keep the other teacher on the other side of the base from complaining."

"Don't worry. He's a Russian. They're tough. And he's really good." I said with a chuckle.

"Ok, I trust you, but how are we going to get him here in time?" Max asked.

"He doesn't live in Russia!" I said with a laugh, "He works in Jean. He's the grave keeper for the military cemetery."

Chapter 21

We pulled up to the cemetery about a minute later in my car and got out.

"Hey, I'm here to see Victor," I said to the guard out front as we walked up. "I need a favor from him."

"Greetings Jack, it has been a while," the front watchman replied in a thick Russian accent. "Victor is over in his tree."

"Thanks Arturo, nice day isn't it," I said as I walked by. Max tried to follow me in, but Arturo closed the gate.

"Let him in Arty, he's with me," I said without even turning around.

We made our way through the cemetery to a large Siberian pine near the back gate. As we got close to it, I put my hand out to stop Max.

"Why are we stopping?" Max asked in a worried yet frustrated tone. "We need to hurry. My class starts in three minutes."

"Then it's a good thing the trip back has no speed limits. Victor!? Are you there? It's Jack."

The tree shook and a large man with several scars across his face dropped out.

"Private Jack, what is it you want?" he said with such a heavy Russian accent that Max had trouble understanding him.

"I'm not a private anymore, and I need you to substitute a class for me old friend. You see I need to brief him on a mission and he needs to teach a class that has driven half of the US subs to retirement within fifteen minutes of the class starting. You know how the American subs are. So I told him you could straighten his class out," I said.

"I'm not sure, what class is it?" he asked.

"It's fixing weapon jams and cleaning weapons."

"OK, I will straighten this class out for you," he said. "But only if I can yell at them as much as I need."

"No problem. I used to yell all the time back there," I said with a grin. "Well, we better get going. Class starts in a minute."

Victor and I raced back to my car with Max trailing behind. We got in and zoomed off towards the base and made it to the classroom with seconds to spare.

"Alright," I said, "Victor is in the room, the kids are coming, we're all set. Let's go to the briefing room."

We went down the alternate hallway so that nobody saw Max out of class, especially not the kids. When we got to the briefing room, I let Max in and closed then locked the door.

"I don't want to be interrupted. This is a very private matter. Don't tell anybody else about this until I give you permission, understood?" I asked.

"Yes sir," he said.

"Good, now we have a huge problem, and what's even worse is that the problem was supposedly executed fifteen years ago. His name is Mario Brazoria, and he was a member of my squad."

"No he wasn't," Max said, confused, "it was you, me, Alex, Jasmine, and at the end your wife Elana."

"Not that squad, my squad from when I was a cadet. It was me, Elana, and Mario under the command of Commander Mikeal Anderson. Then Mario went out of control. He thought he could pull off a perfect crime, like most law enforcement officials do, and then he got carried away. Once he got away with it once, he thought he could do it again and again. Eventually he caught and was executed, or was supposed to be executed I guess. He kept his cover for a while, and he was practically investigating his own murders with us. His murder name was the Hydra because he would kill a set of people, anonymously report the location to us, and then kill twice as many people the next time before tipping us off again. He would also carve a symbol of a hydra in front of where he put the bodies. By the time he was caught he had killed over twenty people. He had had a crush on Elana since the beginning of our squad, and she liked him too, in fact we got along like brothers. So when he was found guilty, it tore us up. I got a phone call from him a few days ago. He said he couldn't wait to see me and Elana again. I could have sworn I saw the man that I thought was Mario smile just before they executed him by firing squad, but I put it off then. Now that I think about it though, he must have been smiling because he wasn't actually Mario. When he was in our squad, he was an undercover scout because he had the innate ability to blend into any situation and he was from a different planet so he could change his face to make him look like someone else just by seeing a picture. I did a little research yesterday though and found out that his kind lose the ability to change faces at his age a year after he was supposed to be executed. I'm working with some friends of mind to take his picture of his original face and use some aging technology to see how it would look now."

  "Well, if this guy was so bad then, and he's probably gotten even worse now, why are you only telling me? Where are Alex and Jasmine?" Max asked with a quizzical look on his face.

"They're not here," I said, "Because I don't want to have their honeymoon interrupted by work like mine and Elana's was. Once they're done, I'll fill them in."

"Ok, but I don't know about this," Max said.

"Don't worry about it. We will be fine on our own.

Chapter 22

The next day I called Elana and Max into the briefing room and once Max finally showed up, he looked extremely pleased about something.

"That Russian friend of yours kept true to his word. Those kids I told you about, well I had them today and they were simply perfect. They were quite and respective, and everyone had their homework done. And I remember at one point one of the troublemakers started acting up and one of his friends said to him, 'Be quiet, or he might take a day off and have Mr. Victor sub again.' I don't know how he did it, but I owe him big-time." Max laughed.

"It's because he's Russian, that's why," Elana and I said at the same time and chuckled.

"Well, anyways, my friend James helped me out and we have a picture of what Mario would look like today if he is still alive," I said simply.

"Then what are we waiting for?" Elana asked anxiously, "Let's go find him. I want to bring this man down and make him pay for what he's done if it's the last thing I do."

"I don't want you to get too caught up finding Mario Elana." I said calmly. "I don't want you to over react and run off on your own trying to find this guy. I hate him as much as you do but we need to focus. We haven't gone off looking for him because we don't know where to look and I don't want to just go running all over the world on a wild goose chase. If we do that, I bet my life he would just follow us around, wait until we split up and pick us off one by one," I finished explaining.

"If we wait, he could kill more and more people Jack!" She responded in a fierce tone that I hadn't heard in a while.

"I don't want you to get carried away! Listen to yourself. You sound the way I did when you were talking me out of killing Van'burke!" I yelled over her.

"I don't want anybody-" she started again.

"I know you don't want him to hurt anybody else, but you need to stop blaming yourself for what he did!" I interrupted. "You couldn't have stopped him."

"Yes I could have!" she yelled at the top of her voice before she burst into tears. "About a month before we caught him, he told me about what he was doing. He told me everything. He even offered for me to join him. I could have stopped him there, but I let my feelings for him get in the way of my mission! I let him go on killing people for a month and if you hadn't caught him, he probably would have kept killing more and more people! Not only that, but three days before you caught him, he sent me a message. He told me that you and the commander were on his next list of targets. That's why he was in your room when you caught him. He was getting ready to kill you!" Elana sobbed as tears continued to stream down her tears in rivers. "I stood by and let him kill all those people!" Elana caterwauled.

I looked at Max and he knew that we needed a private moment. After the door shut behind Max, I turned back around and Elana was still crying her eyes out.

"Elana, you couldn't have stopped him," I said gently. "If you had tried to stop him, he probably would have killed you too. Just let go. Let it all go. I'm here for you sunshine, no matter what happens. What happened then was in the past, and the past is already past. The only thing you can do about it now is stay calm and we can catch him together."

"You would make a great shrink," she said with a small laugh. She was still crying but she was laughing slightly too. I held her tightly in a loving embrace and let her cry into my shoulder. I was going to make everything all better, I hoped.

Chapter 23

The next day Jasmine and Alex finally got back from their honeymoon in Vegas. They were in a great mood until we called them into the briefing room. Once we told them about Mario, it was like they had never been to Vegas in the first place. They were back to all work no playing once more. Every once in a while though, while we were talking, Jasmine would look spaced out and for a few seconds she smiled. I guess she was remembering the fun she had in fabulous Las Vegas. Once we had finished the briefing, we immediately started to work on how we were going to find him.

"What have we done so far to try to find him?" Alex asked.

"We haven't done anything yet because we were waiting for you." Max replied simply.

"What if we send out search teams to every place we've known him to hide in?" Jasmine asked patiently.

"I don't know. He has hiding spots all over the world. We'd be spread pretty thin," I said in an anxious tone.

"We can hit them one at a time. We just have to make sure that the press don't find out about it," Elana suggested.

"Yeah, because if the press find out, then he'll know that we're after him." I agreed. "We have a plan so let's put it into action."

We were all set to leave when I realized something: How were we all supposed to get there without attracting attention? Then I saw the garage. It had two new cars that I hadn't seen in there before. There was a silver Ford Mustang and a jet black Dodge Viper.

"Nice cars guys!" I said in an impressed tone. "I guess you guys are on the government payroll. Let's get going. First stop, San Diego, California. Just follow my car and try to keep up. Last one to the entrance to San Diego has to polish the winner's cars!"

"Oh you're on! Bring it Pops!" Max said the challenge clear on his face.

We jumped into our cars and zoomed off towards 46781 Jackson Street in San Diego. I started off in first and then Alex began to catch up to me.

"I like my car with three coats." he said through the radio.

"I guess you better tell that to Max. Adios boys!" I replied cockily and slammed onto the gas pedal, watching the speedometer needle past 130 miles an hour. I started to pull ahead and I watched as we zoomed past Jean and back onto open desert road.

◆ ◆ ◆

About twenty minutes later, I saw the sign that told me we were now entering San Diego, and I was glad because I was running out of gas and had to use the little leader's room, if you know what I mean. I was still in first, but now Max and Alex were neck and neck. I could hear them arguing over the radio.

"It doesn't matter if you guys beat each other, because you'll still loose to me! Ha!" I shouted into the radio as I entered into San Diego and parked at a rest stop just outside of town. By the time I got back out and filled up my car, I could see them getting closer. Alex was in first now by a few yards. In the end, Alex beat Max and he promised to polish our cars when we got back to the base. Once we all topped off our cars, we started cruising around town looking for Jackson Street. It didn't take long to find it. Once we did, we pulled up in front of the house with the small, rusted numbers that said 46781 and got out. For a second, I thought I saw something in the window, but I shook it off thinking it was my imagination. We knocked on the door and Alex decided to use the oldest cover in the book:

"Pizza delivery, anybody home?" He called.

I knocked again, harder this time and the door creaked open. The room was dusty and all the furniture was covered in plastic wrap. We quickly scanned the room with flashlights and guns drawn, and started to search the rest of the house. Jasmine and Alex went downstairs into the basement, Max started searching the rest of the ground floor, and I went upstairs with Elana. When we got to the second floor, we faced a long corridor with five doors along the side. We looked at each other for a split second and nodded, and started walking towards the first door. We each got on either side and I kicked down the door. We burst in as soon as the door went down guns drawn and flashlights on. We looked around and there was nothing in the room but a window that looked out onto the street below. We found the same thing in the next three rooms and we were about to kick down the fourth door when we heard a crash and a sound that sent us both sprinting down the stairs in an instant with our guns drawn: gunshots.

Chapter 24

We nearly ran into Max on the way down and we all sprinted down to the basement. Once we got down there we found Alex leaning on the wall with a bullet wound in his arm.

"Where's Jasmine?" Max asked quickly glancing around.

"The…window…he took her…Mario took her." He grunted.

"What happened to your leg? It's not supposed to bend like that!" Elana said.

"I was trying to fight him, and I kicked," Alex grunted, "He grabbed it and twisted and I heard a crack. That's when he shot me."

Without another word I was back upstairs and in my car. Elana and Max stayed behind to tend to Alex as I flew out in my Ferrari. Somehow I knew where I was going even though I really didn't have a clue. I followed the road behind the house out onto open road and there I saw a black Hummer driving down the road. I guess Mario recognized my car because as soon as we got onto open road he started to speed up. In no time, I was right next to the Hummer. I couldn't see inside but I knew that Mario wouldn't be driving. I set the Ferrari to go on auto-control and go back to the house. Then, I opened the window and jumped onto the roof of the Hummer and swung into the window and into the back seat, feet first. As soon as my feet broke through the window, I felt them collide with something that I knew was Mario because he had kept his victims on the floor and out of sight. As soon as I could see though, I realized that Mario hadn't captured Jasmine, one of his friends must have. The man I hit with my feet was a short black man. Mario was a lanky Caucasian with a scar over his left eye. As soon as I was all the way through the window, I told the driver to stop without opening my mouth. He knew to stop once he saw the look on my face and heard the click of the chambering mechanism from my pistol that I put against his head. As he stopped, I checked the pulse of the man I had hit and then helped Jasmine out from under the seat. When we got back to the house, Max and Elana were supporting Alex on their shoulders.

"Did you get him?" Alex grunted.

"It wasn't him," I replied. "It was one of his friends, but I have one more idea of where he might be before we start to interrogate him. It's an old base that I visit every once in a while. But before we go, I have to ask you something. Can you swim?"

Chapter 25

What the hell? What kind of question is that? Their face said as they looked at me. The only exception to this was Elana, who instantly knew exactly what I was implying with my question.

"It's not a hard question, so can you?" I asked again.

"Yeah, we can swim. Why?" Alex was the first to ask.

"Because to get to our old abandoned base, you will definitely have to be able to swim," I smirked.

"Why can't we just fly there or take a ship?" Jasmine asked quizzically.

"We can't take any kind of vehicle because the defenses are still active and we'll get blasted to smithereens," Elana said with a broad grin of her own.

"Just tell us where it is already, sheesh," Alex finally grunted.

"Fine, but this will blow your mind. We are going to our old base in the Bermuda Triangle!" I said like a game show host

"No way, we're going to the Bermuda Triangle? As in, THE Bermuda Triangle?!" Max gasped.

"Yes, THE Bermuda Triangle. We have an ancient base in the middle. There is a small island there with our defenses built on the surrounding islands," said Elana. "We can take a boat to a nearby harbor that is about 500 yards away from the island, and then we can try to take a small pontoon boat to about fifty miles out, but then we will have to jump out and swim for the remaining distance. Otherwise we would get blown to smithereens by the short-range defense rockets."

"Alright, are we ready to go?" I asked, which was answered by a mutual nod from everyone. "We just need to get to catch a plane out to Florida. Ready, break!"

After we got to the airport, we went through the stupid security measures that I don't think really help and boarded the next plane to Florida. When we landed, I called in a favor and one of my old friends and rivals got me a speedboat that just cut clean through the water like a bullet through air. We got to one of the nearby harbors and got an old self piloting boat and set it to take us closer to the island but not close enough to get blown to bits.

"Alright, everyone got their scuba gear on?" I asked them. I looked around and they all nodded. "Good. Now, just follow our bubble trail and don't freak out if you see a few sharks. Panicking just draws their attention," I said with a grin. We all jumped into the water and the first thing I heard was Jasmine squeal into the headset: "Jezz this water is cold!"

"Don't worry about it. You'll get used to it. It will feel warmer if you swim towards the bottom." I assured her.

"Really? That's not what I learned."Jasmine grumbled.

"No, but if you swim towards the surface, then you will be detected and turned into Swiss cheese by the laser-guided turrets," Elana buzzed in.

"Alright," I said. "We're almost here. Stick close because just above us is the laser beam grid that can chop you into teeny tiny pieces."

We went a litter farther and then we finally went up. When we came up and saw a large forest with the sun setting dramatically in the background.

"So…where's the base?" Alex asked, puzzled.

"Wow, don't cut the grass for 25 years and it goes crazy!" I joked.

"Well, it's a good thing we were expecting an attack from natives," Elana said as we pulled out our machetes.

We started to chop our way through when I heard a loud hissing noise. Everyone stopped, and I started to look around when a twenty foot snake began to raise out of the vegetation in front of us.

"Um, what is that?!" Jasmine whimpered.

"Ritalin, is that you? It's Jack." I said slowly.

The snake began to lower its head and I and I saw the mark that resembled two pyramids that spiraled all the way down its body.

"His name is Ritalin? Isn't that some kind of drug or something?" Alex asked with a knowing glance at me.

"Yes. The last time I saw him he was about three feet long. I guess this explains the sightings of some kind of sea serpent." I said with a return glance at Alex that said: *drop it.*

"He used to be my hunting pet when we had to look for food when something happened to the supply ships." I explained. "I had Ritalin, Elana had a wild cat named Sam, and Mario had a monitor lizard named Soda Pop. This is great. Now we can ride Ritalin to the base. I guarantee that he knows where it is. Everybody onto Ritalin's back. Try to grab a scale, but don't pull."

Elana and I got on, and then Max, then Alex, but Jasmine still seemed hesitant.

"Come on. Don't worry, he won't bite, I think," Alex said.

"Not funny Alex, but fine." she sighed and she slowly climbed up the side and onto Ritalin.

"I disagree Jasmine, I think it was quite funny." I chuckled. "Alright Ritalin, Take us to the base nice and easy now."

Nice and easy was his last plan though. As soon as I tapped his side, he shot off into the jungle like a roller coaster. We smashed through trees, splashed through a river, and shot over hills until he slid to a stop in front of what looked like a pile of vines.

"Is this your base? It just looks like a pile of grass and weeds," Jasmine said.

"I think this is it. Let's have a look," I said as I jumped off Ritalin.

I walked up to the base, pulled out my machete, and took a swing at the vines. They fell quickly and revealed a smudged metal hatch. I rapped my fist on it and it swung open to reveal a large lizard, standing on its hind legs staring at me.

"Well if it isn't Soda Pop," I grunted.

The lizard snarled and Ritalin began a low hiss in the back of his throat. I pulled out a pistol and they both went silent. Soda Pop crawled out and a tall, slightly plump cat followed and proceeded to jump onto Elana and begin to purr loudly.

"Oh Sam, you've gotten so much bigger. How's my little boy doing?" Elana said in a baby voice.

I went inside and found a light switch. I flipped it and nothing happened, so I turned on my light that was mounted to my pistol, and as soon as I turned it on, I wished I hadn't. There, slumped against the wall of the room, were the rotting remains of my squad leader, and the closest thing I had to a father. There were still globs of dried blood caked to his body and the surrounding walls.

"Who was that?" Jasmine shrieked as she followed Alex in.

"That is what is left of Commander Mikeal Isaiah Anderson. He, he was my squad leader." I said slowly as I removed my hat as a sign of respect.

"But you said that Victor guy was your teacher," Max said slowly.

"No, you goofball, he was our SUBSTITUTE teacher." Elana said with a soft chuckle in an effort to try and ease the tension in the room, laying a soothing hand on my shoulder.

We moved past him and found holes in the wall that I thought were from the fight with Mario. That was until I stood back to try to remember it. When I pointed my light at it, I realized that the marks weren't bullet holes. They were burn marks from a laser.

"You never forget your first," I read out loud.

"What is that supposed to mean?" Jasmine said.

But Elana and I took one look at each other and we had the same thought.

"We need to get to Guantanamo Bay," we said together.

Chapter 26

I shut down the defenses and began to call for a flight team to come and pick us up.

"This is Shadowstar one requesting immediate pickup at my location. The landing zone will be marked by a flare." I said into the radio.

"Ahem. Aren't you forgetting something Jack?" Elana said and nodded towards Ritalin and Sam playing near the runway.

"Elana, I'm glad that we found that they are still alive too, but we don't have time to build a place for them while we solve this case." I said as I lit the flares and dropped them along the runway.

"We can drop them off at our villa in Rome and have a plane fly Victor over to take care of them." Elana argued.

"Fine," I grunted. I pressed the button on the radio, "And a large cargo transport from here to my villa in Rome. Then send someone to pick up Victor Caesar and transport him to my villa as well. Make sure that the large cargo pickup team is good with animals."

"Um, roger that, I guess," the radio squawked.

"There, are you happy now? But I am not taking Soda Pop. I just have a bad feeling about having anything involving Mario."

"Liar, you are nothing, but a liar Jack. I know you still have the necklace," said Elana.

I reached down my shirt and pulled out a small silver necklace with a spiral made of obsidian. Elana reached down her shirt and pulled out a necklace with a slightly smaller spiral, this one made out of pink diamonds.

"I still think we might have a chance with him. Before, I thought he was dead, but now that I know that he is alive, maybe we could have a chance to turn him around." I mumbled.

"I know Jack. I completely understand what you want, but even if we can turn him around, there is no escaping what he's done and as soon as we catch him, he is to be executed," Elana said softly.

"I guess you're right." I sighed. "Well, there's our escort. We better get a move on to Guantanamo. Everybody load up and get on board. Next stop, Guantanamo Bay federal penitentiary."

"Got it." Alex said.

Everyone else got onto the ship and they were waiting for me to board.

"Come on Jack, let's go already." Alex said.

"You go on ahead. I'll catch up later," I said. "There are a few things that I want to check up on around here and I want to make sure that nobody gets hurt when they load up the pets."

"You don't have to make sure they don't hurt them. They can take care of themselves. How could a few animal handlers hurt a giant snake and a jungle cat?"

"It's not the pets I'm worried about getting hurt," I said with a smirk.

"OK, if you say so. Pilot, let's go. Guantanamo Bay, and step on it," Alex said as the doors closed.

As the shuttle took off, I turned and walked back into the base. I walked through the room with the marks on it and up to a wall on the far side of the room and started to feel around on the bricks of the wall. I heard Ritalin as he came in and watched him put the tip of his tail against a set of bricks on the wall.

"You always did remember where the switch was," I said to the giant snake.

I pushed on the brick in the center of where he touched and the wall shook and swung open to reveal a closed hanger. In the center was a large black lump.

"I can't believe it's still here after all these years!" I said as I ran up to the large lump. There was a control pad on the side and I waved my hand over it. The pad lit up bright green though the moss that had grown over most of the screen. The pad beeped and the black lump cracked down the middle with a loud hiss that I knew was the airlock I had installed ages ago to protect the systems. When the black cover finally completely lowered into the floor, I walked up and marveled at the amazing condition that my starship was in.

Chapter 27

I opened up the front hatch, slid into the cockpit, and let my fingers clench and unclench around the controls.

"It's been a while since I sat here isn't it?" I asked Ritalin.

"I'll definitely have to make some adjustments to keep up with the others though. And by catch up, I mean stay ahead of so I don't lose any races in the future." I said with a grin. I flipped the ignition switch and I heard a rumble but no blast which meant that the engine igniter had burnt out. I hopped out and pulled out my sharpening stone that I keep handy for my knives. I struck one of my knives against the stone and it sparked slightly.

"Good. This'll do," I said.

I walked closer to the engine and began to strike my knife against the stone. Eventually I heard a deep rumble and hopped into the cockpit. The hatch closed and I felt the ship begin to slant upwards towards an opening in the roof of the room. The engines fired and I shot out of the building and into the sky. Ritalin slithered out the opening and followed me around as I cruised around the island until I saw the second set of ships approaching it. I landed myself near where the ships landed and watched/helped the soldiers load Ritalin and Sam each into separate ships. I glared at one of them when the soldier tried to bring Soda Pop before Sam got my attention by growling at a handler who was trying to convince him to get into a cage.

"Don't even try private. This cat is as stubborn as his owner. Just shut the cargo door." I said with a chuckle.

Once the pets were loaded onto the ship I went back to my ship and took off for Guantanamo Bay.

When I got close I radioed to the base my identification and purpose for landing there so that they wouldn't open fire as I tried to land on the runway. The landing was a little bumpy but I expected as much for flying something that was a tenth the size of the base after twenty five years without practice. I got out of the ship and followed my escort to the information room. When I got there, I met up with Elana, Max, Alex and Jasmine who were all crowded around a set of files.

"Those the case files?" I asked, causing Jasmine to jump slightly.

"Yeah, it's so big I can't find the beginning though," Elana groaned.

"Oh, wait a second, I think I get it. Here, let me see them," Jasmine said suddenly. "I helped catalog stuff for my parents in their library when I was a kid, and I'm guessing that these files are ordered the same way the membership folders were. That means that the first things are at the front of the folder, but the first folder is at the back of the drawer."

"Oh, there it is then," Elana said, reaching into the back of the cabinet drawer and pulled out a file. "Thanks Jasmine. Now, let's see. The first recorded hit made by the Hydra was found in the top floor of the Ostrog Memorial Tower in Yakutsk, Siberia. I guess that means we're going to Siberia then."

Just so you know, there's a reason Elana is saying that Ostrog is in Siberia and not in Russia. From 2080 to 2083, the area of Russia considered to be Siberia revolted against the rest of Russia, which had since become communist again. In our never-ending fight against communism, the United States sided with the democratic Siberians and the final result was Siberia receiving complete independence from Russia.

"Good thing Victor insisted on teaching me Russian. I can translate for us when we get there. But before we go, I have to make a quick stop at the base to pick up some parts. I don't want to deal with any more annoying pat-downs. I won't take long. I just need a new engine igniter set," I said.

"Why do you need a new engine igniter set?" Elana said.

"Come outside and I'll show you." I said with a grin.

Chapter 28

The first thing that any of them said was "wow!"

"Jack, you really had to get your ship?" Elana asked, her tone showing that she was slightly irritated but couldn't help but chuckle.

"Yes, yes I did." I replied with a goofy grin.

"So, you need a new engine igniter because this one was ruined by corrosion that was a result of the humidity of the island?" Alex asked.

"Exactly," I answered bluntly. "This way I can skip the stupid airplane security measures and get there ahead of time to plan out everything. I just have to give clearance on arrival." I said.

"Well just go to the base and meet us at Yakutsk Airport, ok?" Elana said.

"OK. Will do." I said.

◆ ◆ ◆

Once I took off, I flew quickly over to the base to replace the igniter, after nearly getting shot out of the sky by the defenses I had designed myself, and then I arrived in Yakutsk about an hour later and checked into a hotel for the night. Then the next day I was waiting at the airport when the others arrived around noon.

"Alright, stick close to me and don't wander off. You have no idea what to say to get these people's attentions and they are very snappish when it comes to Americans."

"Got it," They all answered with a nod.

We left the airport and I hailed a taxi to the Memorial Tower.

"So what now?" Alex asked as we stepped out of the cab at last.

"The report said that five bodies were found on the top floor with a hydra symbol carved in front of them, so up we go." Elana read off her SixthSense device. Being the one who was always prepared for everything, she had obviously scanned the case file, or at least the report for the crime in question.

"But where are the elevators?" Jasmine asked innocently as we entered the building and passed the security checkpoint inside.

"This building was built at the end of the Siberian Revolution in honor of the Siberian soldiers who died fighting for their independence, and it was based on a really old kind of fortress." Elana chuckled.

"I don't get it. Are the elevators hidden in the wall or something?" Jasmine whined.

"Hun, there are no elevators. We have to take the stairs. All twenty seven stories of them." Elana laughed.

"Race you to the top!" I laughed as I started sprinting up the stairs.

"You're on Jack!" Elana said with a giggle as she took off in pursuit

"Ugh, stairs?! Why?" Jasmine groaned.

"Don't worry Jas, just climb on." Alex said, crouching down in front of her.

"You're the best baby!" Jasmine squealed with delight as she climbed up onto her husband's broad back to ride piggyback up the flights of stairs, Max ran after them in an effort to keep from being left behind.

◆ ◆ ◆

Ten minutes later, Jasmine and Alex finally made the top to join the rest of us. The only thing near the stairs was a large wooden door with a pair of ornate wooden handles.

"Alright, let's get going. Everybody ready? Weapons locked and loaded?" I asked habitually.

"Yes sir." They replied quickly as they pulled out their pistols.

"Good, now I'll open the door and as soon as I do, I want you to rush in guns drawn and make it clear that we're here."

"Understood sir." They responded.

I opened the door and they rushed in as soon as possible and announced our presence. I came in after them and the door slammed shut. We looked around the room, which was lit by several sets of candles on the walls around us with no other doors or windows. The first thing I heard was someone clapping slowly.

"Nice entrance Jack." An old voice echoing from the shadows that filled the room around us boomed.

"Show yourself Mario." I shouted.

"Oh, you're Mr. Tough guy now. And how are you Elana? You look simply amazing in body armor. And this must be the Shadowstar squad I heard about. I assume that Jack already told you guys that we used to be in a squad." The voice chuckled.

There was a blur and the candles went out. In an instant I felt a prick in my shoulder. Naturally, I swung, but my fists just met nothing but air. I heard Jasmine scream and I turned on my light to see a figure in a dark tattered cloak hunched over Jasmine. I fired. The cloak groaned and disappeared again. I heard the door slam and held my light up to see Jasmine.

"Team, sound off!" I shouted into the darkness as I carefully began to review Jasmine's injuries.

Jasmine was covered in slashes that were bleeding horribly. There was nothing but silence. I pulled out a flare and lit it. All around me my team lay bleeding on the ground. Max had a bloody nose and several cuts on his arms. Elana was slumped against a wall, her torso covered in lacerations and a deep slash running down her left calf that was gushing blood. Alex sat with his back against a wall unconscious, his right hand and face obscured by blood from multiple places. I pulled the heavy doors open, jammed it with a torch, and carried them down the stairs one by one as fast as I could, shouting in Russian for an ambulance the entire time. I was hit with a terrible shock when I realized why Alex's hand was so bloody as the ambulance finally pulled up with several police hovercars right behind: It wasn't there.

Chapter 29

The next day I went to see my team in the hospital in Yakutsk. Everyone else had suffered from internal bleeding and required emergency surgery on arrival at the hospital. What I couldn't understand was what that prick on my shoulder that I had felt was, or why that was all the attacker, who I was sure must have been Mario, had done to me. When I looked at it the previous night, it had looked like a puncture wound from something like a syringe or a hypodermic needle of some sort. But when I had the doctors check my blood stream, they said there was nothing wrong. So I sat there in the large room waiting for one of them to wake up. I needed to know that it was ok. Eventually they each woke up. Elana was the first one to wake up, and then Max was next, then Alex and Jasmine, who seemed to wake up at the same time somehow. There were no words to describe how it was when Alex woke up and discovered that his hand and his wedding ring were gone. For a moment he just stuttered and stared at the heavily bandaged stump at the end of his left arm.

"What happened to my hand!?" Alex finally managed, then repeated louder and louder "What happened to my hand! Why is my hand gone!? Where is our ring!?" Alex continued shouting over and over again.

"Alex, I'm so sorry. He caught us off guard." Elana said, sounding defeated and weak.

"My ring, my whole fucking hand, is gone! And it's your fault!" he shouted at me.

"You're right. It is my fault." I grumbled.

"If you hadn't chosen to chase after this nutcase, then I would be at our new house watching TV with both my hands right now!" He continued.

"If I hadn't called you to join us, then you would probably be six feet under with no body at all! He would have already killed you by now!

That's what he does. He goes for people that I care about to drive me insane. And you yelling at me telling me the obvious is not helping. Now if you want to see where you would be right now if I hadn't called you two to come along, then that can be arranged!" I roared as his constant berating caused anger to replace my original feelings of guilt. My yelling was so loud that a nurse rushed in to figure out what was going on.

"Mr. Marr, please calm down or I will have to escort you out. Getting Mr. Griffin's blood pressure and heartbeat up will not help his recovery." The nurse pleaded.

"Don't bother. I was leaving anyways." I growled and stormed out of the room and to my ship.

"I'm going to where I can think, and fix my ship. Don't come looking for me." I said in a recorded message on Elana's phone.

Then I took off with two stops in mind. First, I was going to Shadowstar base to pick up supplies for my ship. Then I was going to my Villa. I needed to be with someone who had been through this before. I needed to go see Victor.

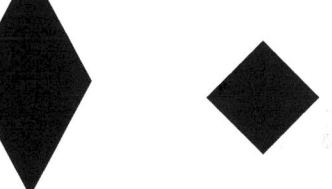

♦ ♦ ♦

I finally landed in front of my Villa to a greeting party of three. Victor and the pets were waiting for me just outside the front door.

"Hello Jack. So what is it that you had to talk to me about?" Victor asked.

"I don't know what to do Sir." I said. "Every time that I feel like I'm doing the right thing, somebody gets hurt. I can't stand to lose someone to him. Not again. If that happened, I don't think I could go on living. So, can you help?" I asked as I popped open the hood of the ship's engine compartment.

"Well, young Jack, I'm not sure I can help you with this case. This man is very, how you say, slippery." Victor said slowly, trying to find the right words to use.

"Well, since you're here, would you mind helping me fix my ship?" I asked.

"Gladly. If I remember correctly, fixing things and flying could always lighten your mood." Victor chuckled as he walked over to join me behind my ship. "But, where is the rest of your team?" He asked, puzzled.

"In a hospital in Siberia. And I'm pretty sure I just lost two of the members. Hang on, my phone is ringing." I said.

I pulled the phone out of my pocket and looked at the caller ID. It just said "unavailable."

"Hello?" I answered somewhat apprehensively.

"Hello Jack. I hope everyone is recovering well." Mario said promptly.

It was like I was a stick of dynamite and he was the match that just lit the fuse.

"What do you want now you worthless piece of shit!?" I exploded, yelling into the phone. "You took everything from me once, and now you want to do it again! Tell me where you are. Let's finish this once and for all. I want to make sure you burn for what you did and I want to be the one standing there with the lighter when it happens." I shouted into the phone.

"Well that's not very nice. By the way, I know you're with Victor. Tell him I said hi. And by the way, I'm--" and then he hung up.

"Who was that Jack?" Victor asked as I stood up and walked back towards my ship again. "Where are you going? Didn't you want to fix the plane?"

"I don't need to fix it where I'm going. I know where he is and I want to finish this. Do not come with me and if my 'team' comes by and wants to apologize, then tell them that I wasn't here." I said.

Then I got into my ship with Mario's old 'catchphrase' in my head: "Life is like a Ferris Wheel, because it seems like fun at first, but if you stay on it, then it just goes around in the same place every time forever."

Chapter 30

I shot across the Sahara desert and landed near a small village in Mali. I was just stepping out of the ship when I heard motorcycles coming towards me. I looked to the left and approaching the village from the opposite direction that I was headed was three small sand clouds. As they got closer I realized that the sound of motorcycles was getting louder, so I ran. I ran out towards a small abandoned village that was about five miles from the village that I had landed near. The motorcycles kept coming closer and I heard Elana shout from the middle cloud.

"Stop Jack! Where are you running to? Just stop and we can talk about this." Elana yelled over the roar of the engines.

Then she pulled in front of me and stuck her hand out to grab my shirt. I grabbed it and flipped it and her off the motorcycle.

"What is this about? Why are you all the way out here in the middle of nowhere? He called you didn't he. He called me too. You can't beat him on your own. You're not even armed!"

"I am out here alone because I need to end this here and now. We can't just walk around and wait for him to attack us again. Last time, we lost a hand, next time we won't be as lucky. I need to do this and I need to do it alone! So just leave now!" I shouted angrily.

Then without stopping for a reply, I sprinted off towards the village, the location of Mario's second body pile in the original case. I looked back and saw that they had all jumped off their motorcycles. Alex had a wad of bandages around his hand stump and Jasmine was limping slightly. They weren't running after me or chasing me on their bikes. They were just walking slowly behind me like some normal stroll, la de da de da. So I slowed and they caught up to me. The whole time they were silent. None of them said anything until we got to the village. We made our way to the center of town where we saw a large black silhouette of a pyramid. As we got closer, we realized something that was simply horrifying. The pyramid was made of heads of the villagers. It was so sick and twisted that I almost lost my lunch right there on the spot. Then, I felt a rush of adrenaline and my vision seemed to begin to have a red-orange tinge around the corners. I turned as I felt the prick in my shoulder again to see Mario, standing there in his cape. He was grinning ear to ear.

"YOU!" I howled as I swung hard at him. As my fist collided with his face, he flew back and disappeared. Then he ran at me from the side and hit me. I swung again and he seemed to teleport right as I hit him. Then he was behind me and he jumped onto my back. He tried to put me into a sleeper hold, but I grabbed his head and threw him off. He hit the ground hard and moaned loudly. Then my vision clouded over and I couldn't see. I felt several people jump on to me and I hit the ground. As my vision cleared, I heard a click and felt metal restraints tighten around my wrists. I looked around and realized that Mario was gone. In his place lay my squad was covered in bruises and marks, as well as a few reopened wounds.

"Wait, where's Mario? He was just here in front of me!" I asked wildly.

"What are you talking about Jack?" Elana asked, her voice filled with confusion, "What is wrong with you anyway?! Why did you just attack us all of the sudden, and why is your shoulder turning black?"

"I just saw him. I was fighting him, my shoulder hurt, and I don't know what happened." I stuttered.

"No you didn't just fight him. What you did do is suddenly attack us for no reason whatsoever. I mean, I understand that you are mad at us, but there are easier ways to solve a problem then by hitting it."

"That's what it was! It was a neurotoxin! That's what the prick was. And, it probably had some kind of nanotechnology in there too. Wait, I can't feel my shoulder. And my elbow is burning!" I gasped.

I looked at my arm and watched as my skin slowly turned jet black to my elbow. I flicked it, and felt nothing. I hit it, and still felt nothing.

Chapter 31

"It's killing your nerve endings, and therefore killing you!" Elana said.

"Thank you Capitan obvious! You see! I told you to stay away from me and now you know why. I figured he had something planned and now he is taking over my body." I shouted. Then I pulled out my phone and dialed the base.

"Hello, its Jack. I need to book an appointment with Dr. Jeffery Stiles. I'll be there soon. Bye." I said and hung up.

"I need to find out how to get rid of this. So you guys go find something to do. Just stay off of this case. Alex, now you can go and watch all the TV you want. I hope you're happy. And watch your back." I said. Then I hopped in my jet and shot off to Constellation Division base.

◆ ◆ ◆

When I got back to the base, I hopped out, went up to the medical deck, and waited for Dr. S. who finally came out to find me about ten minutes later.

"OK Jack, let's have a look at, wow! What did you do this time!" he said as he looked at my arm, which was darkening by the second.

"Come with me Jack. I want to get a better look at what's going on. This reminds me of something I saw a while ago." He said.

We went into an operating room where I lay down on the bio-bed and after the doc finished typing a few quick commands into the monitor, the scanner ring moved up and down the length of my body a few times, and when it finished, the monitor beeped and Doctor Stiles gasped at what he saw.

"What is it doc?" I asked.

"There are at least twenty, no, thirty growths of some kind in this section alone and they seem to be spreading very quickly. They are forming on top of the nerve endings and separating the signal between two endings. Looks like they're nanobots that are actually controlling the signals. I was afraid of this." He groaned.

"What were you afraid of?" I asked nervously.

"This is a new weapon we only just discovered recently. We called it SICK, which stands for Sadistic Impulse Controller and Killer. It's a disgusting combination of bioterrorism and nanotechnology, been used to try and make sleeper agent, only it didn't really work as well as a secret when the skin started changing colors, but forces still continued using it due to the psychological effect that the skin color change had." He explained quickly. "We will have to surgically remove the bots."

"I need you to operate immediately so I can get back to work." I said, though there was somewhat of a reluctant tone in my voice.

"Well, I can be ready in about ten minutes." He said. "If you want, I can call your team-"

"No! Don't you dare!" I shouted.

"OK, OK, keep your blood pressure down." He said calmly. "I won't call them, but I have one question."

"Ok, shoot." I said reluctantly.

"What do I do if they are already outside?" He asked curiously.

"What! How did they find me! Did you call them already?" I asked angrily as I craned my neck to see the team standing in a window looking down from the waiting room.

"No, no, no. I promise I didn't!" He insisted with his hands raised innocently.

"Fine, just put me under now before they come in so I don't have to listen to them complain. I'm in a very bad mood right now in case you haven't noticed." I growled as I lay down on the operating bed and stared at the ceiling.

"I completely understand. Sweet dreams Jack; I hope they are better then what you've been telling me about so far." He said. Then he put the mask over my face, I heard the hiss of the gasses being released and I let the warm, calming darkness of sleep overtake me.

Chapter 32

At first, I saw a grey smoke for the floor like I did when I died, but I knew that I hadn't died, or I was at least pretty sure. Then I saw a flash in the distance and as I walked towards it, I saw a silhouette of a person and as I got closer, I recognized the shape. When I got close enough to see the face, my assumptions were confirmed as I stared at Commander Anderson.

"Sir," I said, "What are you doing here? Did I die again?"

"No Jack, you're still very much alive. I heard that you were having trouble and I wanted to help, so what's the problem kiddo?" He asked with a slight chuckle.

"Well, sir, it's Mario. He's back. And I don't know what to do. I've tried tracking him down and all that's happened is that the people closest to me got hurt, just like the last time. One of my teammates even lost a hand, along with his wedding ring. So, what should I do?" I pleaded, slightly winded from the long explanation.

"The first thing you should do is take a long, deep breath and relax. You are too tense. That's how Mario got to you before. He made you freak out and overstress about some things and because of that, forget other things. Second, you need to put more trust in your teammates. They are not the enemy, so you need to stop treating them like it, but don't baby them either. And most importantly, you need to put more trust in yourself. You can do this. You just need to believe that you can. Do you understand now Jack?" He finished.

"Yes, I do. Or at least, I think I do sir." I sighed, relaxing slightly as I realized the reality of what Commander Mikeal was saying. "I have been putting too much pressure on my team and I, I know what I have to do to fix it. Is that all sir?" I asked.

"No, now that I think of it. You need to go see Victor. Tell him to engage plan Markoff in case there is more than we think going on here. If he asks how you know about it, just make up an excuse. You were always good at doing that." He said with a chuckle. "That is all Jack, you are dismissed. Happy hunting!" and with those final words, he faded back into the smoky wall and disappeared.

There was a bright white flash, and I was back in the operating room, but I wasn't in my body. I was hovering near the ceiling of the operating room. In the window to the left I could see my team with their face pressed against the glass trying to see my body through the crowd of surgeons around my body. I realized that all but one of them were interns that were watching my surgery! Then I looked over and saw that my arm was cut opened and all over the muscle were tens of small black dots. Then, as I got closer, I saw a flash in the doctor's eye and I knew that he was determined to finish this operation with a success. In the blink of an eye he removed the remaining dots that were on the arm muscle and sutured the incision. Then he wrapped in a bandage and pulled his hands back like a cowboy who had just hogtied a bull. Then I felt myself being sucked into my body, there was another bright flash, and I woke up in the recovery wing with my squad standing around me.

"Welcome back Jack, how was your nap? Are you feeling any better?" Elana asked sincerely.

"Yeah, actually, I can feel my arm again." I said.

"Good, because I wouldn't want sympathy to ruin this moment!" Elana yelled, her tone changing on a dime from concern to sheer fury. "What in the word were you thinking Jack! Just running off and leaving us like that!"

"I thought I knew what was best, but now I understand that I was wrong. I know what I have to do now, and I need your help to do it. Please, I know I was wrong for doing this and I'm truly sorry. Now, first thing we need to do is get out of here. I need to go see Victor." I explained as I began to sit up.

"Fine, but I want to show you something we did while you were out." Jasmine said with a snicker.

"What did you do? How long was I out?" I asked, confused.

"About two days." Alex said in a flat tone, refusing to look up at me, and I couldn't blame him.

"What!? Two days!? Why didn't you wake me up?" I asked, slightly irritated now.

"Because the doctor wouldn't let us. He said that the most important part of recovery is rest. And he knew if you were awake soon after the operation, then you would go charging out the door with no more than 'put it on my bill.'" Elana said. "So he increased the strength of the anesthetics so that you would stay asleep."

"Okay, I guess that makes sense. Let's go. Hurry up and show me what you want to show me already." I insisted as I stood up slowly and turned to follow them, already dressed in my regular clothes.

"Ok, it's in the hanger bay. Come on out." Max said with a cocky smirk on his face.

We left the recovery ward and made our way to the hanger. As soon as we got there, I knew what they wanted to show me. In the hanger were three ships that I had never seen before, all lined up in a row and bearing the same ID tag on the wings that were identical to the tag on my ship's wing.

"You guys made your own ships? Really? Why?" I asked.

"This way, you can't run away from us by just jumping in your ship and flying off." Elana said smugly.

It was pretty easy to tell whose ship was whose. Elana's looked like a replica of mine but with a silver paintjob instead of black. Alex's was bright red on top and was much larger than the others. It had thicker wings and several cannons mounted both to the wings and the ship. Max's was a design that seemed similar to a Night Fox, but slightly larger and better armored.

"Nice ships guys. I just hope there are no hard feelings about before. I mean, I know that it's a lot to ask considering what I put you through, but, I'm really sorry." I said.

"We know Jack, you've said that a thousand times already!" Jasmine said with a smile.

"Alright then, let's get to work and end this for good!" I said. "Everybody load up, top off, and get ready for takeoff! But before we go chasing after Mario again, I have to go see Victor. I had a vision and I'll fill you guys in on the way. But Alex, how do you plan to fly with just one hand?" I asked.

"Easy," he said, "I don't." then he held up what would have been the stump of his missing hand. But, instead of seeing a stump, I saw a regular human hand.

"It's amazing what they can do with prosthetic limbs these days, isn't it Jack?" he asked

"Yeah, it sure is amazing. Well, how's about we go solve this problem once and for all? Who's with me?" I asked.

"I'll follow you anywhere Jack, and you know that." Elana said.

"And don't forget that we always have your back, sir." Jasmine said proudly with a grin.

"Well then what are we standing around for then? Let's get to work!" I shouted. "Everybody load up and prepare for takeoff!"

Chapter 33

    We loaded up and took off within the next ten minutes. Once we were in the air I spent the rest of the flight explaining what Anderson told me to do.

    "I wonder what "Plan Markoff" is." Alex said.

    "The Commander always talked about something Markoff," Elana said ponderingly. "He said that Markoff was this man that lived back when he was a cadet, I think."

    "Yeah, and I think he said that Markoff was a serial killer who, killed I think over a hundred people." I said as the story from so long ago beginning to return to me in bits and pieces.

    "Yeah, I remember now! He said that Markoff was executed and put in a museum of historic criminals. And, they say every year, on Friday the Thirteenth, his ghost comes and haunts the museum." Elana said.

    "Yeah, you're right." I said. "And if I remember correctly, the Commander told us that story every night after Mario went rouge. I think Plan Markoff has something to do with stopping dangerous serial killers."

    "Well, why don't we ask Victor about it since we're here?" Alex said.

    "Wow, that ride went by fast." I said as we landed and hopped out.

    We walked up to the door and tried the handle. We expected it to be locked, but it wasn't. I knew from that moment that something wasn't right. I slowly opened the door and peered in. I saw Victor sitting in a chair, facing towards the door, and shaking his head as he noticed us. As usual, I didn't listen to him. We pushed the door open and the first thing I saw was a large shadow flying towards me. It landed on top of me and I realized that it was Soda Pop. I pushed his head back with one arm and pulled out one of my knives out of my thigh strap with the other. I put my knife close to his throat and pulled back the arm that was holding him back. He pushed forward instinctively and ran his neck into the knife blade. He squirmed for several seconds as his throat began gushing blood, and then went limp.

"You killed him! You killed my friend! I'll destroy you for that you bastard!" I heard Mario shout from the entrance to the other hall.

He dashed at me like a wild dog. In a second he was jumping towards me, eyes wide and pupils dilated to little pin-pricks in his eyes. He had a maniacal grin and was giggling like a madman. He had a large sword in his hands with a plasma ring around the rusted blade and he was thrusting towards me as he approached. I quickly drew my own sword, turned on the energy ring, and swung at him to make him back up as I stared into his eyes.

"Let's do this the old fashion way. No guns, no energy rings, just blades. Me against you. Nobody else involved, no tricks up the sleeve, no nothing." I said calmly, my gaze unwavering.

"You're on Jack. I guess you forget that I was always better than you at sword fighting. And once you're dead, I'll destroy your friends. And I will love the whole thing. You remember how you said you wanted me to burn for what I did? Well I think it will be the other way around. The only difference is that you won't burn alone." He said with a psychotic grin.

"I used to think that if I caught you and talked to you, then I would be able to convince you of what you did and help you. But I see know that you are too far gone. I see now that the best we for me to help you, is to end you." I said, staring him down.

Then I took up a fighting stance with my sword and waited for an opening. As if we were sharing thoughts, we charged each other at the same time and clashed in the middle of the room. I shoved him back and continued to attack him with blow after blow. He barely had time to block one hit after another. I figured that he was getting close to an adrenaline rush so I knew I had to end this soon before his adrenaline gave him an advantage. I struck him again and quickly shook the handle of the sword, releasing the second blade so that it unfolded from the sword and created a dual-bladed sword, my weapon of choice. We sprang apart and then clashed again. This time, I spun my sword around and knocked his sword out of his hand. Then I kicked him to the ground and moved in for the final kill. Just as I was about to end it, he pulled a knife out of his pocket and swung, barely missing me. He jumped back onto his feet and grabbed his sword again. He swung again and this time I could tell that his adrenaline was building. I made a decision and quickly twisted my blade before flipping it up into the air along with Mario's.

"I thought I could end this honorably, but it has to end now." I said. He was about to respond when suddenly, his eyes went wide and with a final grunt, dropped to the ground and died, the swords hitting the ground behind him at the same time with an echoing clang.

It happened all so fast that I doubt anybody saw it. While I was talking, I pulled out two small partially serrated knives attached to each arm with a mechanism. Before he knew what was happening, I dug one knife into his liver and the other into the side of his neck to slice through both his carotid artery and the jugular vein, causing severe blood loss and near instant death. I stood back to look at that body lying in a quickly growing puddle of blood that used to be my teammate, friend, and the closest thing to a brother I had had. Then, I felt a sudden wave of exhaustion and blacked out.

Epilogue

    I woke up the next day in the recovery wing and was released with advice to take it easy for the next month or so. But, as you have already probably figured out, I have a problem with listening to orders, so as soon as I was given the OK, I walked calmly out of the medical wing, and then sprinted to my garage to grab a set of tools. I spent the next two months working at night with a group of ten of my closest friends aside from the squad and then slept through most of the days. When I was working, it was on something under a large tarp near Jean, and nobody aside from me and the ten friends I was working with were allowed inside. When I finished, I piloted several Death Falcons in and unloaded them under the tarp for the next three days, and the next day I used the loudspeaker in the base and projected it out to the town.

    "May I have your attention please? Will everyone please make their way to the large tarp just outside of town? Thank you." I said, and then sprinted down to the tarp so that I could meet everybody there.

    Once everybody was there turned on the mike and got their attention again.

    "Thank you for coming here ladies and gentlemen, and now, I give you our newest tour attraction: The military animal training facility, which is also a zoo for the public!" I shouted as I pulled off the tarp.

    Everybody was amazed at the beautiful zoo that had been put together. Everyone stood up and began cheering at the top of their lungs.

    "Well, Jean, go check out your new zoo!" I said and immediately people began to rush in through the gates.

    I felt good watching everybody enter the zoo. I felt almost like I was required to do something for this little town after all it did for me. But that is another story for another day.

The End

Author's Note

  Hey, it's me, Jesse Carr. Kinda obvious since I'm the author and this is the author's note, but that's not the point. The point is that I just wanted to take the time to personally thank you for reading this novel. I put a lot of emotion, effort, and A LOT of time into this book. I also put a lot of myself into this. Now, my hope is that you didn't just read a little bit of the beginning, then read the last two or three pages or something. I figure that is still gonna happen, but I just hope it doesn't, at least not very often. Funny thing though is that if you just read the first few pages, and then read the epilogue, you're gonna be really confused. The epilogue is really more related to book two, which I can assure you is on its way. I know that whenever I'm reading a series, my biggest annoyance is when I read through a book and am stuck waiting months or even years for the next one. But I can't release the next one too soon or I won't be ready for the next next one. One last thing, if you have any questions, comments, suggestions, or even if you're looking for someone to chat with for advice or something, feel free to email me at shadowstarsquad@gmail.com. Obviously, that's not my personal email address, sorry to disappoint you. I'll answer any messages as soon as I can, but please don't freak out if it takes me a while. Well, that just about wraps everything up. Thanks again for reading, and keep an eye out for the next adventure, *Falling Titans*. JC

Made in the USA
Lexington, KY
11 September 2014